ECHOES
OF
ZERO

ECHOES OF ZERO

Ross H. Spencer

ST. MARTIN'S PRESS • NEW YORK

By nature we are all prodigals but a few of us become exceptionally adept at the game. When our mirages prove to be hot air we come home, if there is someone to come home to.

I did . . . . . and there was.

ECHOES OF ZERO is dedicated to Shirley Spencer.

Ross H. Spencer

Copyright © 1981 by Ross H. Spencer
For information, write: St. Martin's Press,
175 Fifth Avenue, New York, N.Y. 10010
MANUFACTURED IN THE UNITED STATES OF AMERICA

Design by Mary A. Wirth

10 9 8 7 6 5 4 3 2 1 ·
First Edition

Library of Congress Cataloging in Publication Data

Spencer, Ross H
    Echoes of zero.

    I. Title.
PS3569.P454E3   813'.54   80-29354
ISBN 0-312-22552-0

I realize, when in my mirror's presence,
That I am in my second adolescence;
I seek new loves and flattery beguiles me,
It matters not what sort of wench defiles me.
Ah, second adolescence, thus accursed,
You've treated me exactly as my first.

Ross H. Spencer

The third Thursday of May 1968 was warm, slightly overcast, and memorable. The Soviet Union had just agreed to build an $800 million industrial project south of Cairo, the AFL-CIO had just kicked the UAW's ass into the street, and I was drinking Clinch Mountain with Red Collingsworth at Longo's Bar across from the Globe building.

Nothing memorable there.

I usually drank at Longo's Bar.

With or without Red Collingsworth.

Red was a used car salesman but we were still friends.

We had done three seasons together at Philadelphia before

the war. I was in the war and I liked the war better than Philadelphia.

Red wasn't in the war and he liked it better, too.

I wanted to talk about the '39 and '40 seasons. Red preferred '41. In '41 Red had hit .346 and I had hit .252.

Red wasn't quite that good and I wasn't quite that bad. Red had enjoyed one of those crazy summers. Almost everything he hit took a bad hop or somebody fell down trying to field it. '41 just hadn't been my year. In a twin-bill at New York I whacked six consecutive screaming line drives.

Right at somebody.

The first five were turned into double plays, and when Russ Williams started a triple play with the sixth, the crowd gave me a standing ovation.

Damned good thing it happened in New York.

I'd have been lynched in Philadelphia.

One Sunday in Pittsburgh I came up with the bags loaded and I busted one about eighteen miles down the line. A pigeon came along and knocked it foul.

In Philadelphia somebody would have shot the pigeon.

That was the only time I ever really missed Philadelphia.

It was extra good to see Red that afternoon because the Bannister case still bothered me and Red helped get it off my mind. Old ballplayers tap the same vat used by old schoolmates and old soldiers. Not a bad grape in the barrel.

We never missed getting around to the fat widow who had gone bananas over Red, and the time she and Red got stuck in the doorway of the men's room at the Cyclone Tap on Broad Street, with her trying to get in and Red trying to get out.

Or when she hired a private detective just so she would

know where Red had been drinking. When Red heard about it, he paid half the freight because he wanted to know, too.

Or the night we'd spent in the gypsy camp. We still talked about that. So did the gypsies, I daresay. The last I heard Red still couldn't play that goddam mandolin.

Red was a nice little guy but he had one very irritating habit. When he got drunk, he got hungry. This time Red wanted to go to Big Mike's on Wabash for ribs.

I told him I'd rather drink.

Red went for ribs and I ordered another Clinch Mountain, and got back to the Bannister business.

And points beyond.

The trial had been over for two months and it hadn't changed a thing. Martin Bannister was dead as a doornail, Eloise Henderson was free as a bird, and I was drunk as a skunk. Sam Cohen winced at that kind of talk.

Sam was editor at the *Globe* and he said that good reporters always steered clear of trite expressions. That didn't bother me a hell of a lot. Nobody had ever accused me of being a good reporter. Especially Sam Cohen.

Sam hadn't hired me in the first place.

Martin Bannister had hired me long before he retired. Bannister was a patriotic cuss and I was an ex-ballplayer who got into a collision with a Jap hand grenade on New Georgia. The war was raging and reporters were difficult to find. When Sam Cohen looked at some of my stuff, he announced that it was no longer difficult to find reporters.

He said it was impossible.

I didn't try to write fancy. I just called a spade a spade and turned it in. I wrote two seasons of baseball. My blunt style worked just fine and I had a hell of a good time. Then Pete Nelson came back from the war and I got bumped onto the plum assignments. Society balls and charity drives and high school gymnastic meets.

I even reviewed an opening performance of *Tosca*. I reported that it was a dead-ringer for the Battle of Iwo Jima, only this time we lost.

Mack Hadley was editor then and he wouldn't run it.

When Sam Cohen took over as editor, things got worse. Much worse.

In March of '68 Sam sent me to the Loyola Field House to cover the Midwest Kennel Club's Obedience Trials. In the parking lot a Doberman tried to emasculate me. He didn't miss by much. I hadn't climbed a telephone pole in thirty-five years, but it came surprisingly easy.

When I came down I got drunk. I found a pet shop and bought a muzzle. I went back to the Loyola Field House and put it on the guy who owned the Doberman. That got the *Globe* a lawsuit and me a one-month suspension. I wondered why they didn't fire me.

Then Eloise Henderson's trial came up. Muggsy O'Hara had been scheduled to cover it for the *Globe*. On the eve of the trial, Muggsy went to the wake of a guy named Finnegan.

5

There was a bit of drinking. On his way home, Muggsy had it out with a Tulsa Overnight Express full of Marsh-O-Nut candy bars. Muggsy lost.

So did I.

Sam Cohen pulled me out of mothballs and sent me to Eloise Henderson's trial.

That would have been the beginning.

If the beginning hadn't been twenty-seven years earlier.

In January of '41 the *Chicago Globe* had held its Annual Midwinter Baseball Banquet. It was a miracle that anybody from Philadelphia was invited. The A's had finished last in '40 and the Phils had finished laster. Or lastest. Whichever it was, we ended up fifty games back. But that had been better than '39.

In '39 it had been fifty and a half.

The Philadelphia writers made a very big to-do over our improvement.

They noted that if we continued to come on at our breakneck pace we might very well be pennant contenders in one hundred and one years.

'40 had been my second season with the Phils and it was a good one. I hit .301 with twenty homers and thirty-two stolen bases. They said I had exceptional outfield range and a rifle arm. When you get right down to it, there were only a few reasons I didn't make it to the '40 All-Star Game in St. Louis.

Medwick, J. Moore, Nicholson, Ott, and West.

In alphabetical order.

Red Collingsworth and I received banquet invitations. I'll never know why Red accepted, but they didn't have to ask me twice.

My mother had passed away in May and I was alone in the old house out on Creek Road. The holidays were over, the weather was rotten, the pool room had just burned down, and Susie Weatherby was closing in like a panzer column.

Susie visited me every day. She kept the house tidy and she did my laundry. I appreciated that. What I didn't appreciate was all the starch in my shirt collars. I said, "Sooz, these collars make me feel like a Saxon serf."

Susie yawned.

I said, "A man could get his goddam throat cut this way."

Susie kept right on starching my collars.

A couple of years earlier, Susie and I had gotten friendly at a New Year's Eve party. We had gotten so friendly that we celebrated the arrival of '39 in Room 3 of the Trojan Motel in Floydstown. It had been a very active celebration.

At the height of the festivities Susie had moaned, "Oh, there'll AL-ways be an ENG-land," and "A HORSE, a HORSE, my KING-dom for a HORSE!"

Later I had said, "Sooz, what the hell were you talking about?"

Susie said, "Oh, gracious, I don't know, just anything that

came to mind." She kissed me and added, "Did it disconcert you?"

I answered, "Well, I got to admit that the business about that horse didn't do much for me."

Long before dawn Susie had discovered that we were made for each other. She said, "Rip, we were made for each other." This left only one question unanswered. *When would we be married?* Susie asked me the only question left unanswered several times each day.

I made vague replies. Like, "How's about three months after the Battle of Armageddon?"

Susie had a different timetable. She always wanted to get married within the hour. She would say, "But I'll compromise. Let's make it next week." Or she would attack from another angle, asking, "How would you respond if I told you I was pregnant?"

I would say, "I'm not sure. How do heart attack cases usually respond?"

When I accepted the banquet invitation Susie said, "How long will you be gone?"

I said, "Sooz, I really can't say. Sometimes these affairs drag on for days." I stared out at the cold, gray Ohio sky. I said, "Even weeks."

Susie said, "Heavens, I never heard of a banquet lasting that long."

I said, "My gosh, Sooz, some of those Roman shindigs went on for months."

t had been the standard affair. Soup or salad.
Weak or wilted.
Chicken or roast beef. Raw or burned to a crisp.
Mashed potatoes and gravy. Both lumpy.
Ice cream or jello. Melted or rubbery.
Coffee. Lukewarm.
Introductions. Glowing.
Applause. Half-hearted.
I was the last to be introduced.
The master of ceremonies said that I was an up-and-coming
youngster who would strike terror to the hearts of National
League pitchers. I don't think Bucky Walters attended the

banquet. If he did, he wasn't listening. Bucky struck me out thirteen times in '41.

By ten-thirty Red Collingsworth was slightly drunk. At ten forty-five he got his left eye blacked by Mush Watson of the Cardinals.

By eleven-thirty Red was plastered and he wanted a rematch. He went looking for Mush Watson. Since nobody had remembered to wear baseball uniforms to the banquet, Red mistook Ralph Watson of the Senators for Mush Watson of the Cardinals. Ralph and Mush were brothers. They looked much alike and both were shortstops, but there was a difference in their fighting styles.

At eleven forty-five Ralph Watson blacked Red's right eye.

Late that evening I stood at the bar nursing a bottle of Pabst and clawing at my starched shirt collar. I listened to the bartender whistle "Careless" over and over, and I tried to think of a way of escaping the clutches of Susie Weatherby. With some semblance of dignity, of course.

Prior to this I hadn't known Martin Bannister from a busted bale of hay. Then he sauntered up and put out his hand. He said, "I'm Marty Bannister and I own the *Chicago Globe.*"

I didn't know how to respond. I said, "Well, I'm Rip Deston and I just bought a '41 Buick Century."

Bannister laughed a hearty, rolling laugh. He told me that he had followed my baseball career closely and he proved it by reeling off a bunch of figures that didn't matter much to me. He knew my slugging average, my fielding average, and how many runners I had cut down at the plate. In my book all that mattered was batting average, runs batted in, and homers. Bannister said that he liked my aggressive, heads-up style of play and that he had looked forward to meeting me for a very long time.

It was an odd remark. I had played in the majors for two years and I was with a rotten ball club located seven hundred miles from Chicago. I attributed his approach to drunkenness, because Bannister was red-eyed and he carried a water glass sloshing over with whiskey. He asked if I'd do him the honor of sitting at his table and shooting the bull. He said that there would be just the two of us. I told him that I wasn't the world's champion conversationalist. Bannister winked and said, "That's just fine because I plan to do most of the talking anyway."

He was about fifty then, a square-jawed, Florida-tanned, self-assured, energetic man. I got the distinct impression that Bannister wasn't accustomed to being refused.

He escorted me to his table and waved for drinks. Right off the bat he wanted to know all about me. I said that there wasn't much to tell. I told him that my father had been killed in the fighting at Meuse-Argonne before I was born and that I had lost my mother in May. He was silent for a time and then he asked about my childhood. Had I known poverty?

I told him no, my mother and I had lived comfortably because my father had invested wisely. Bannister beamed approvingly, and we moved from topic to topic. Baseball, Joe Louis, Roosevelt, Lana Turner, and back to baseball.

The party rolled along. Some of the guys were singing

"Sweet Violets." At twelve-thirty Red Collingsworth lurched by. At twelve forty-five Archie Walsh of the Pirates busted Red's nose.

Bannister's wife was living then and he spoke lovingly of her. He told me about what she meant in his life and of her great understanding. By way of making conversation, I said that one must possess great understanding before he can recognize great understanding.

Bannister looked up quickly and a smile twitched at a corner of his mouth. He said, "Well, that's one hell of an observation, but I'm not sure it will hold water."

I said, "Neither am I, but I think it must be like a blue jay knowing the difference between a wild turkey and another blue jay."

Bannister broke into his big laugh and said, "Well, by God, I think I've just met another blue jay."

Bannister wasn't as drunk as Red Collingsworth, but he was drunk enough to offer me a job. He said, "Rip, you'd make a fine newspaper man."

I squinted at him.

"You're smart, you have hustle, and I like the way you say things. You speak in color."

I replied, "Mr. Bannister, I have trouble writing a grocery list."

Bannister pointed a finger at me pistol-style. He said, "There, that's exactly what I mean. Now your buddy Collingsworth wouldn't have put it that way. He'd have said, 'Hey, I can't write.' "

I answered, "Hey, he can't write and he can't fight either."

Bannister said, "Rip, newspaper reporting is little more than getting to the point in as few words as possible. You seem to have a knack for that."

Red Collingsworth staggered and fell into our table. Bannister paid no attention. He went on, "You could get a good run at the business during the off-season months."

While I was looking at my watch I told Bannister that I'd think about it.

It was one-thirty.

What I was really thinking about was getting Red Collingsworth out of there before he got killed.

Bannister didn't miss any of our Chicago ball games in '41. He always wore a Philadelphia baseball cap and he sat in the first row at the west end of our dugout. He waved his arms and cheered if I so much as scratched my ass.

He took me to dinner several times that year. Nice places with dim lighting, ankle-deep carpeting, soft music, and white telephones brought to the tables by men in tuxedos. Like in the movies.

He kept the pressure on. He said, "Look, you can run with Maruzek on the crime beat, and I'll see to it that you work with Pete Nelson on football and hockey."

I said, "I'm not sure I can do it."

Bannister snorted. He said, "Of course you can do it. You're an absolute natural. Just watch, listen, and learn—and get paid while you're at it."

I put him off. But not too far off. I said, "Would sometime after the first of the year be okay?"

Bannister grinned like a great white shark in a YWCA swimming pool.

We shook hands on it.

We finished the '41 season fifty-seven games off the pace, and I got drunk with Red Collingsworth for three days. Or it might have been four. In Philadelphia you can hardly tell.

Then I went back to Cornelius, Ohio.

Susie met me at the Erie station in Floydstown. She was driving her father's '37 Packard. There must have been something wrong with the steering. It's five miles from Floydstown to Cornelius, but Susie drove seven. We were all over the highway. When we reached my house out on Creek Road, Susie took a box from the backseat. She said, "This is a nice chocolate cake for your welcome home party."

Susie put the cake on the kitchen table and we went straight to bed.

In practically no time she was moaning, "How BEAU-tiful HEAV-en must BE!" and "Hoo-RAY for the red, white, and BLUE!" and "Oh, welcome HOME, Rip, Rip, RIP!"

We never did cut the cake.

spent Thanksgiving afternoon at Susie's house. Susie's mother was dead and Susie cooked dinner for herself, her father, and me. Her father was a dour, no-nonsense type. He was a church deacon and he watched me the way a hungry cat watches a canary. After dinner he cleaned and oiled his double-barreled shotgun.

Susie walked out to my car with me. She said, "Rip, I'm afraid your welcome home party got me pregnant."

I groaned and said, "Aw, come on, Sooz, how many times does this make?"

Susie said, "I'm pretty sure it's for real this time."

I said, "Have you seen the doctor?"

Susie said, "Doc Phillips?"

I said, "I guess so. He's the only doctor in town."

Susie put her hands on her hips. She said, "My God, Rip, are you utterly insane? Doc would tell my dad and my dad would murder me!"

I said, "The hell he would. He'd murder me!"

The Japs bombed Pearl Harbor two weeks later and I damn near sent Hideki Tojo a thank-you card.

I sold the house to the Merriams on Monday morning and my car to Bud Strong on Monday afternoon. I caught a bus to Columbus on Monday night. I enlisted in the army on Tuesday morning.

Rip Deston. Patriot.

annister wrote to me steadily during the war. He always used stationery that had a blue jay in the upper right-hand corner. He said that his job offer would stand for as long as he owned the *Chicago Globe*. He said that he was proud that I had picked up a gun and gone to war instead of hanging back to play baseball with an over-privileged military team. He never failed to throw in a few lines of patriotic poetry. Bannister was a flag-waving sonofagun.

While I was doing my six-month stretch in the hospital, I took a rhetoric composition course through the Armed Forces Institute. It was called English 101 and it came from the University of Chicago. My teacher's name was Sophia T. Ellsworth.

Following the third assignment I received a note from Sophia T. Ellsworth.

She cautioned me against superfluous use of trite expressions.

There had been nobody at the receptionist's desk on that windy, gray morning in March of '44. I limped unannounced into Bannister's walnut-paneled office. Bannister studied some papers at a desk that could have doubled as a carrier deck. The gray in his hair was more pronounced now, and the furrows in his face were more deeply etched.

He looked up and blinked. His jaw dropped. He said, "Well, I'm a dirty sonofabitch!"

He bounced from his big leather chair and came around the end of his desk like a good halfback who sees a sliver of daylight. He gave me a roughhouse swat on the shoulder and a bear hug. Then he noticed the cane. He said, "Aw, no!"

His voice broke and he said, "Aw, goddammit to hell, no!"

I said, "It's only temporary."

There was a long, difficult silence that Bannister managed to break by clearing his throat loudly.

I said, "I believe you said something about a job."

Bannister nodded. On his way back to the desk he whipped out a hip-pocket handkerchief and blew his nose. He flopped into his chair and said, "You want to take a shot at baseball?"

I said, "That's about all I know."

Bannister grabbed a telephone. In a moment he said, "Rich? . . . Rich, I have your new baseball writer up here . . . . . . Oh, yes, you do, Rich. You just haven't been aware of it, that's all . . . . . . I know, Rich . . . Yes, I know that, Rich . . . Sure, Nelson's coming back. But right now he's in the goddam Solomon Islands . . . . . . Well, give Wade a raise and put him on something else . . . Oh, racing, maybe . . . Any kind of racing, Rich . . . Uh-huh . . . Well, how about archery? . . . Mmm-hmmmm . . . Badminton? . . . I see . . . Look, Rich, I'm busy, so just find another job for Wade, will you? . . . . . . Rip Deston, that's who . . . Deston, Rich . . . D-E-S-T-O-N, that's how . . . . . . Why, Rich, Deston would have been the greatest goddam player in the history of the game . . . . . . Sure, sure, all those homers but he didn't have Deston's speed . . . Ty who? . . . Oh, him . . . . . . Philadelphia, that's where . . . The Phils, Rich . . . . . . Well, Jesus Christ, Rich, you can't blame Deston for that . . . . . . Certainly he can write it, he played it, didn't he? . . . . . . Why, of course it has something to do with writing it . . . . . . Well, all right, Rich, I'll tell you why—

Because I just happen to own this goddam newspaper, that's why! . . . . . . Thanks, Rich, you've been very cooperative . . . . . . Wait a second and I'll find out."

Bannister covered the mouthpiece and glanced at me. He said, "Can you type?"

"Fifteen words per minute with one finger."

Bannister yelled into the phone, "Sure, Rich, he can type."

He banged the phone down. There was fire in his eyes. "When I promise a man a job he gets a job."

He popped to his feet and said, "Let's go to lunch."

From Bannister's private elevator we walked the two blocks to Angelo's. My leg was weak, but I made it without using the cane. Bannister did a lousy job of not noticing how I was doing. He kept such a close eye on me that he nearly fell over a fireplug. When he regained his balance, he grinned it off. He said, "They ought to be more careful where they put those goddam things."

Angelo's was a cozy little flat-roofed joint with empty chianti bottles hanging all over the place and the aroma of spaghetti sauce heavy in the air. It had bright red tablecloths and its wallpaper made up a huge interior view of the Roman

Coliseum. Our waitress was an attractive blonde in her mid-twenties.

I eyed the wallpaper and said, "When do the lions come out?"

The waitress yawned, "The very moment we find a Christian."

I glanced at Bannister. I said, "I think I'm in trouble."

Bannister grabbed the waitress by the hand and pulled her to him. He threw an arm around her and chuckled, "Rip, meet Clancy."

I said, "Clancy?"

Clancy answered, "My father wanted a son. My sisters' names are Kevin and Rory."

It developed that Bannister wasn't very hungry. It also developed that I wasn't very hungry. Bannister lunched on vodka martinis and I had Clinch Mountain. We talked. The war and the newspaper took up the early going. Bannister gave baseball a very wide berth. He could see that my playing days were over.

We listened to a fat accordion player do "Sorrento."

I kept tabs on Clancy. When I couldn't see her, I could hear her.

She was a fast, efficient waitress but she banged dishes, clinked glasses, and cussed like the top-kick of Company B. She was obviously a very tough little broad but she was interesting. She was put together like a million dollar race horse.

The fat guy played "O Sole Mio."

I said, "Look, Mr. Bannister, how did you ever become interested in a Philadelphia ballplayer?"

Bannister raised a words-of-wisdom finger. He said, "It was because of a play you didn't make."

28

I asked, "Which one was that? I didn't make more plays than I did make." I was beginning to feel the Clinch Mountain.

Bannister answered, "It was in '39 and you guys were in town losing 9–1 in the eighth."

I said, "Our pitching must have been just a bit sharper than usual."

Bannister continued, "Lieber lined one into left-center and you tore up about twenty yards of real estate trying to make a catch that wouldn't have made the slightest difference to anybody."

I said, "It would have made a difference to Lieber."

Bannister smiled, "Sonofabitch!" He whacked the table with his fist. "Right, goddammit! That's a viewpoint I can appreciate!"

When Clancy walked, her hips swayed like willows in a summer breeze.

The accordion player did "Oh, Marie."

I whistled a bit of the last chorus and said, "I sure like that Italian stuff."

Bannister said, "She isn't Italian, she's Irish." Bannister was drunk, too.

His wife had died in an automobile crash some six months earlier and our talk drifted to her. And then to women in general. If you can generalize women. I'd be the last man on earth to recommend it.

The accordion player took a break and Bannister said, "How are you doing with the ladies?"

I shook my head. I said, "I'm the great All-American out. Shot-up veterans don't make it big in the romance league."

Clancy brought another round of drinks. She put her hand on Bannister's shoulder, "Marty, you'd better ease up on the sauce."

Bannister said, "Get out of here, you shanty Irish shamrock!" He tried to swat Clancy on her backside, but she was too quick for him. She made a face at Bannister and left.

Bannister went on, "No girl friend?"

I answered, "None whatsoever."

Bannister said, "Well if I were you, I'd have a hack at Clancy. They tell me she's hotter than Kelsey's kitchen."

I said, "There was a girl back in Cornelius, Ohio, that I really cared about, but she was dead-set on getting married."

Bannister grinned, "Most of them are. What was her name?"

I answered, "Susie Weatherby."

Bannister said, "By God, that's the perfect name for a girl from a town called Cornelius, Ohio."

I went on, "Sooz was driving me nuts. Every time I turned around she told me she was up the creek."

Bannister frowned, "Sometimes they aren't kidding." He wiped out his vodka martini with a gulp. He said, "I met a beautiful girl during the first war, when my wife was in Chicago and I was in a backwoods army camp." Bannister sat tight-lipped for a few moments. Then he said, "Well, you know how it goes." He missed our ashtray by six inches. He ground his cigarette stub into our bright red tablecloth.

Clancy appeared with a scowl. Bannister glared at her. He said, "You got some kind of problem?"

Clancy said, "No, but you do. That goddam tablecloth is going to cost you four dollars."

Bannister leaned back. He grinned, "Hell, it'll be a pleasure! I never did like red anyway!" He hoisted his drink and looked rather pleased with himself. He said, "My favorite color is blue. What's your favorite color?"

Clancy stepped back. She said, "Marty, you're crocked! Your eyes look like a couple gopher holes and you ask an Irish gal what her favorite color is!" She went away shaking her head.

Bannister turned to me, "Now where was I?"

I said, "At last report you were in a backwoods army camp."

Bannister thought it over. He said, "Impossible. I haven't even been drafted yet." He lapsed into silence. Then he said, "Clancy is right. I'm bombed. I think I better blow this firetrap." He grabbed my hand and shook it. "Check in with Rich Morrow sometime this week and he'll make arrangements to get you to spring training." He threw some money onto the table and stumbled out.

The fat accordion player strolled in from the lounge playing "Vesti la Giubba." I sat there pushing my drink around. Clancy came by. She leaned over until her hair brushed my cheek. It was soft and there was a clean fragrance about it. She said, "Don't worry about Marty. I called the *Globe* over an hour ago and his driver was waiting right out front." She giggled, "It happens at least twice a week."

I started to get up.

Clancy said, "Don't you dare move. I get off in half an hour."

Clancy nibbled on my shoulder. She said, "How would you like to have a hickey?"

I asked, "How much are they?"

Clancy said, "The first one's on the house."

Clancy was generous. She gave me two hickeys. She said, "By the way, you were number two thousand six hundred and eighty-four. Also two thousand six hundred and eighty-five."

I said, "That's an awful lot of hickeys."

Clancy said, "Not hickeys, dammit. Times. I keep a log."

I said, "So did the captain of the Titanic."

Clancy said, "I have my heart set on twenty thousand."

I sat bolt upright in Clancy's over-sized bed. I said, "Well,

33

this may come as a very great shock to you, but there is absolutely no way you are going to make it tonight."

Clancy said, "I'll make it before I'm ninety if I don't get sick."

I sagged back to my pillow and covered my eyes. I said, "My God, what an outlook."

Clancy said, "You'll be a big help."

I said, "If I don't get sick."

Clancy ran a gently inquisitive hand southward from my navel. She said, "You want to try for the hat trick?"

I said, "Look, Clancy, I just got into town and I'm not oriented and I was wounded in the war and I haven't recuperated and I think I've lost my car keys."

Clancy said, "You told me you don't have a car." She poked me in the ribs. She said, "Let's have a cup of coffee while we're waiting."

Clancy was a fireman's widow with a pension that would last until she remarried. Clancy had no intentions of remarrying. She was five-five, peroxide blonde, hard blue-eyed, passionate, profane, good-hearted, and loud. When Clancy whispered, buildings shook. She was one of those people who sincerely believe that the vociferous will inherit the earth.

She was at her noisy best in the kitchen. There she became deafening disaster. Clancy opening a can of soup was like ten drunken Apaches barbecuing a buffalo. Alive. Her dishes were cracked and her pans looked like demolition derby fenders. In ten kitchen minutes Clancy could wreak more havoc than all the howitzers of history.

Clancy probably learned how to cuss while in the womb. She knew every nasty word ever coined and she had made up a few of her own. Clancy swore at cloud formations, telephone poles, and dandelions. She cussed in her sleep.

She was crazy about potatoes au gratin, tight dresses, professional football, and sex. Of these, sex was the winner in a romp. Clancy would say, "If I wasn't supposed to use the damn thing, how come God gave it to me?"

I would say, "Yes, but I don't believe He expected you to wear it out so soon."

Clancy may not have been the most jealous woman who ever lived, but she was certainly the most suspicious. She believed the worst of everybody. Especially me. If I was civil to a barmaid, Clancy put it down as the beginning of a torrid love affair. If I helped a ninety-year-old blind woman across the street, Clancy figured I was putting the make on her. If Clancy had been half-right, I would have been nothing but elbows and eyeballs.

But somehow we got along.

For twenty-four years.

Martin Bannister retired in January of '61. He said, "Rip, I'm going to let up on the accelerator and give somebody else a chance to bust his ass."

He took a long trip. He was away for more than eight months and he was a much different man when he returned. Sober, quiet, distant, seemingly introspective. The last time I saw him was in early '62. He was white-haired then. Frail and weary. He said, "Pete Nelson will be throwing it in shortly and that's when you get your baseball job back. I've made very firm provisions for that."

I said, "It isn't important."

Bannister said, "Yes, it's important but not as important as

37

the wealth of knowledge you've gained writing everything from soup to nuts."

I asked him what he intended to do with his time. He told me that he planned to live quietly and do some writing. "I've always wanted to write," he smiled wryly. "It's a bit late in the ball game."

He wished me luck. There were tears in his eyes. And mine. I thanked him and I meant it. He had been a hell of a friend to me.

The management of the *Globe* fell temporarily under the control of a supervisory board, and a hatchet man was brought in from Boston. Heads rolled in all directions. Augie Blesch and Saul Tanner were fired on the spot. Rich Morrow took a big demotion and Mack Hadley quit. Sixteen reporters got their walking papers, but somehow I held on. Sam Cohen moved up to the editor's desk.

I heard that Bannister had taken a young mistress. He bought a fourteen-room house with a rooftop garden on five acres in the Stone Manor section of Surrey Hill.

The news of his death hit me like a hand grenade explosion.

I am a bona fide expert on hand grenade explosions.

Henny Dugan had broken the story in the *Beacon.*

"Late last night Martin Bannister, millionaire owner of the *Chicago Globe,* descended from the rooftop garden to the patio of his palatial residence in north suburban Surrey Hill. Martin Bannister had done this on any number of previous occasions but this time he didn't use the stairs."

I didn't get beyond that. I went out looking for Henny Dugan.

I found him at Mexican Joe's on Wells Street. He was wearing his customary carnation and drinking his usual margarita.

I poured his usual margarita into his coat pocket.

I stuffed his customary carnation into his ear.

I said, "That's for the funny line about the death of a damn good man."

Henny said, "Aw, Rip, that's just my style." He was pale. He said, "You know, sardonic and all that old jazz."

I walked over to Longo's and got barreled.

By the manual of human relations, Eloise Henderson figured to be Martin Bannister's principal
heir. She had lived with him for something like six years and if
relationships of that type don't deteriorate rapidly, they tend
to get thicker and thicker. Six years was the proof of a pretty
fair pudding.

There were a few points that required clearing up and Ace
Burke of the *Post* had attended the preliminaries. According to
Ace it had been Eloise Henderson's responses to questioning
that started the pot boiling. He didn't think she came on as she
should have. Not that she'd been rude, short-tempered, or

sharp-tongued. But she'd certainly been matter-of-fact, down-to-earth, and pragmatic. Ace had a habit of saying things in threes. He figured that if you missed the first two you could still grab the caboose.

Eloise Henderson said yes, she had been with Martin Bannister just before he died. Was there something wrong with that?

Yes, there had been an emotional discussion that evening. During their years together there had been many emotional discussions. Never mind about what.

Yes, she had been in her room when Bannister plunged to his death. Listening to the radio, if it was anybody's business. She didn't think it was.

No, she didn't know every detail of Bannister's will. She assumed she would inherit something. It had been part of their agreement. Never mind what agreement.

Yes, she had loved Martin Bannister. Never mind what kind of love.

No, she hadn't pushed him. My God what a question. It was insulting and utterly unworthy of reply.

All right, enough of this nonsense.

Indict me or let's go home.

It took some doing and it required a stupidity above and beyond that customarily exhibited by public officials, even in the State of Illinois. Perhaps the tide had been turned by whispers of a missing witness, a gardener who had seen something that night. Or by the report that a laundry maid would be willing to testify concerning a serious squabble she had overheard shortly before Bannister's fall. Whatever the reasons, a few imbeciles got together, glued opportunity to possible motive, multiplied by vague rumor, came up with considerably less than nothing, and indicted Eloise Henderson for the first-degree murder of Martin Bannister. She was released on bond and a trial date was set. Which made about as much sense as me getting involved in a Kentucky Derby.

I didn't have a horse and the state didn't have a case.

loise Henderson was nothing but guilty. I had that gut-twisting feeling. Somehow she had lured Bannister into that rooftop garden and pushed him off. Two adults in their right minds hadn't been out there looking for roses in the middle of the winter. The setting was unique, but there was nothing original about the action. Cheap young bimbo wipes out aging sugar daddy. It happens all the time.

I sat in the back row during the trial. No close-ups for me. I wanted the panoramic view.

Eloise Henderson was defended by Stuart Richmond, Bannister's own lawyer. A cunning, stunning psychological ploy. I supposed she had swung that deal with a tasty blend of money and flesh. Richmond was a portly graying man with the wild eyes, the rumpled brown suit, and the oratorical delivery of a rural fire-and-brimstone evangelist. His legal reputation was awesome and he wasted no time in living up to it. He demolished the prosecution's presentation the way a Sherman tank crushes a one-hole outhouse.

The courtroom accommodated some one hundred people. Three-quarters of them were there on behalf of Eloise Henderson.

Servants described Miss Henderson's infinite tenderness with the failing Mr. Bannister, her devotion, her monumental patience, her reading to him, playing his favorite recordings, lighting his cigarettes, and attending his every need.

Bannister's business associates wept as they told of Bannister's great admiration for Miss Henderson, of his unswerving faith in her, of how she had brightened his fading years, and made his life a rhapsody of joy unsurpassed.

In well-drilled ranks the soap opera parade passed in victorious review and I got the feeling that Eloise Henderson might be canonized then and there.

Meanwhile, the prosecution blundered helplessly around the arena. Its star witness hadn't made it. The gardener had left for the Los Angeles airport in the company of two men who wore dark blue suits and gray hats. He had turned up dead in an alley. Just another mugging, of course.

Yep.

In desperation the prosecution turned to the eavesdropping laundry maid. Oh, yes, she said, there had been a very heated argument between Miss Henderson and Mr. Bannister. Their voices had been raised and ten minutes later Mr. Bannister had crashed to the patio.

Stuart Richmond smiled disarmingly at the maid. He noted that she wore a hearing aid. Had she worn it on the night of Bannister's demise?

The maid said, "His what?"

Richmond said, "Demise."

The maid said, "I never knew he owned one."

Richmond said, "His death."

The maid said, "There must be something wrong with this hearing aid."

Richmond nodded sympathetically.

The maid said, "Mr. Bannister wasn't queer if that's what you're driving at."

Richmond said, "Were you wearing your hearing aid on the night of the tragedy?"

The maid said, "No, I couldn't find it because I lost my glasses."

Richmond said, "How did you hear this violent argument without your hearing aid?"

The maid said, "They was just hollering something fierce."

Richmond said, "What were they hollering?"

The maid said, "I couldn't tell without my hearing aid."

Richmond said, "Perhaps they weren't hollering. Perhaps they were singing."

The maid said, "Well, if they was singing it must of been grand opera."

The judge was nearly in hysterics. So was the jury.

It was a farce and I sat through it wire-to-wire.

I watched Eloise Henderson. She was fascinating. Like a deadly reptile. I marveled at her. She wasn't much over twenty-five. How could she kill as she had killed, endure what she was enduring, and maintain the icy calm she was maintaining? I considered her massive potential for cloak-and-dagger work. Here was a female with the potential to eclipse Mata Hari's fabled exploits. She was far lovelier, twice as ruthless, and three times as clever. Mata Hari had paid the great price. Eloise Henderson wasn't about to go that route.

Simplicity is the essence of beauty and Eloise Henderson knew it. She wore the bare minimum of makeup. She dressed unaffectedly. Simple dresses and plain three-inch heeled pumps. Her only bow to self-adornment was a conservative pair of black pendant earrings. Onyx, possibly.

Over the days I came to learn and anticipate her mannerisms. Her sweet, frank, bright smile that vanished almost before you saw it. Her perplexed little-girl frown, so innocent that you had to wonder if she knew about the birds and bees. Her tapping of an earring causing it to swing rhythmically. Certainly not a nervous habit. It seemed to accompany periods of deep thought.

She gave the impression of wide-open sincerity. She was on excellent terms with the English language and she used it as deftly as a surgeon uses a scalpel. She spoke gently, warmly, and persuasively in a voice that belonged in every bedroom in the world. It was a voice I would have recognized in the depths of Hell.

She displayed no belligerence, but she was nobody's patsy. A woman's tears present a formidable defense, but Eloise Henderson spurned a shield of such transparency. She stood straight and tough and she parried the prosecution's thrusts with the skill of a Vienna fencing master.

She and Richmond kept piling up the points. The farce became a rout and the outcome was never in doubt.

Still her vast composure held my interest.

Somewhere beneath that placidly beautiful exterior there had to be a woman capable of laughter and tears and I found myself wanting to know more about her.

I had never met a murderess.

It was ten-thirty on a cold, cloudy night.

Clancy squeezed up close to me and said, "I think I'll make it. That was eight thousand nine hundred and thirty-six and I still got forty years to go."

I said, "Is that right?"

Clancy said, "Well, say something, will you? Say it was good or say it was lousy but say some goddam thing."

I said, "Clancy, you're always good."

Clancy said, "Rip, you're all wrapped-up in this goddam trial. You don't know whether your ass is punched or bored."

I said, "They'll turn that little bitch loose sure as Cain scragged Abel."

Clancy sighed. She said, "Well, all right, here's one for you. Skoobie Dix was in for lunch today."

I said, "The cabbie?"

Clancy said, "Yes, and Skoobie met a man that Eloise Henderson used to live with."

I popped up like a jack-in-the-box. I said, "Who, for Christ's sake?"

Clancy said, "A guy named Jiggs Argyle who owns the Stumble Out Inn at Armitage and Albany."

I started to dress.

I said, "Clancy, call me a cab, pronto!"

Within ten minutes I was in the backseat of a Checker assembling a portrait of Jiggs Argyle. He would be a darkly handsome bastard with sleek black hair and manicured nails. He would wear a diamond ring, Italian suits, and alligator-skin shoes. He would be suave and witty and I would probably punch the sonofabitch right in the mouth.

The Stumble Out Inn would be a dim, sexy joint with plush booths, carpeted floors, lush music, and waitresses wearing satin shorts, black net stockings, and spike heels.

I got out of the cab in a light drizzle.

Wrong every inch of the way.

The Stumble Out Inn was a gaunt frame building much in need of repair. Its interior was austere with bare floors and battered booths and faded World War II cuties curling yellowly on cracked walls. A lopsided jukebox belched "Orange Blossom Special" at the top of its frayed lungs.

Jiggs Argyle was a good old greens and cornpone downhome boy wearing a dirty T-shirt, ragged blue jeans, and beat-up sneakers. He was bald, snaggle-toothed, and overweight. I was his only customer and he said, "Name your poison, partner. If I don't got it, I'll go somewheres and git it."

I threw a twenty onto the bar. I said, "Clinch Mountain and get in yourself."

Three drinks later Jiggs Argyle was chattering like a magpie. He said he batched it upstairs. He said he pulled a fair-to-middling afterwork trade. Construction men and factory hands, mostly. He said night business was slow because the neighborhood had gone to hell and it had become a fine area for getting your head bashed in.

Jiggs rattled on and I listened. My mind just couldn't accept the picture of the exquisite Eloise Henderson in bed with Jiggs Argyle.

In a few minutes I asked about her.

Jiggs said, "Who?"

I said, "Eloise Henderson. The woman who's on trial for the Bannister murder."

Jiggs said, "Oh, yeah."

I unbuttoned my coat and threw the switch on the little tape recorder in my pocket.

Well that may of been her name only I never knowed her by no Eloise nor no Henderson neither. She was just plain ole

Pennsylvania Woods to me, only I always called her Pennsy.

Used to live right around the corner and come in here a lot of afternoons. Back maybe '61 I reckon. She was only like twenny give or take a mite, but she had what they call poise iffen you know what I mean. Smarter than a forty-dollar buggy whip but never spoke much till she got spoke to. None of this here rattle-brain jibber-jabber like you git from mostest wimmen. Even dressed quiet, iffen you know what I mean. She was a gal what you would of been proud to of taken home to ma. That's how come it damn near decked me when I found out she was a stripper.

She never made no bones about it. You asked Pennsy a question, you got yourself a answer and you could taken it or turnen it loose, iffen you know what I mean. But you just knowed she wasn't going to be no stripper forever on account of she was just too damn purty for that. She had that short honey color hair and them big blue eyes and that pert little ole nose and I gonna tell you them lips was right outten somebody's rose garden. She was built like you damn well better be built iffen you figure on taking off your clothes and making any money at it. She walked like some kind of prize panther but she never flaunted herself none. Leastwise not in here she didn't.

I reckon I went a little goofy about her. You know how a guy can git knocked flat on his ass by a purty thing less than halfen his age. She was working at Abe Golwitz's Golden Garter up on Wilson Avenue, but I never went in that joint till she moved over on Magnolia and didn't come in here no more. I got kind of lonesome for her, so on Wednesday nights I'd git Harry McNabb to watchen the place and I'd take me up to that Golden Garter to see Pennsy do her thing. Firstest time I was there I kind of apologized and said I didn't want to embarrass her or nothing. She just give me that little ole quick smile of hers and said something as to how I wasn't seeing nothing the whole damn world hadn't already got a good look at.

Abe Golwitz run that there Golden Garter just like all the other strip places from here to Halifax. The ladies got up on the stage and waltzed around till they got as naked as the law would allow and then they come down in the crowd and circulated and gotten them suckers to pop for champagne cocktails what didn't have no champagne in and highballs what never got near a bottle of booze. Pennsy used to sitten with me most every time I come in, and I'd buy her a whole mess of them there fake drinks and we done us some talking.

Turned out Pennsy was from Pennsylvania somewheres and she come to Chicago to make it on her own only nothing didn't worken out right so she become a stripper to keepen the wolf outten the smokehouse and you can't hardly blame her none for that on account of a body got to eat.

I seen me some strippers in my day, but ole Pennsy won all the marbles. She had this here knack of looking real bashful-like and there was nights she had about two hunnert guys just a-climbing them walls.

What turnt it all around was ole Abe Golwitz always getting on her back about her stripping faster so's she could spend more time hustling the customers. I come in there one night whilst she was stripping and soon as she gotten done I seen ole Abe corner her and he was just awaving his arms and carrying on like he was John Flip Sousa or somebody. When Pennsy gotten loose she come over to my table and she was smiling real sweet but her eyes had a glint like that ole Georgia sun bouncing offen a Winchester barrel. She setten down and asked would I be so kind as to buy a round and swappen drinks with her.

Well Pennsy knocked off a few hookers of the real stuff and I gargled me about a pint of Lipton's tea afore Abe come up and caught her and man he read her the class double A riot act. He tole Pennsy next time he seen her drinking on the job she was all washed up and he said he was going to clock her and from now on he wanted to see her G-string in just a couple minutes not by the middle of next month.

He was meaner than a crock of cottonmouths and I was gonna hang one on his whiskers, only Pennsy give me a look not to. She throwed Abe one of them there little red robin hood smiles and she said she would do a whole lot better next time, just wait and see.

Pennsy up and marched backstage whilst that big redhead name of Firehouse Phyllis was still peeling and soon as Phyllis got finished the band swung into "Pennsylvania Polka" which was Pennsy's coming on song, since she was from Pennsylvania and everything.

They must of played it through three times and Pennsy didn't show and Abe Golwitz was fixing to go backstage to see what was the matter when all of a sudden them there curtains got ripped open and out stepped ole Pennsy nakeder than a baby Georgia gator, and oh, man, you should of heard the roar what went up. Only people what wasn't cheering was Abe Golwitz and that pair of vice squad cops at the bar by the name of Kurowski and Laird.

Pennsy gotten arrested on the spot and so did Abe Golwitz

55

since this was back in the days when galloping around stark raving naked wasn't exactly the thing to do even in Abe Golwitz's Golden Garter.

I went down and bailed Pennsy out and she gotten in my car and said as how she sure hoped that was fast enough for Mr. Golwitz and I tole her iffen it wasn't she shouldn't fret none, since there wasn't hardly no way she could of gotten it did much quicker.

Pennsy was flat-ass busted and she didn't have no more job and Abe wouldn't pay her what he owed her, so I brungen her here till she come acrost something else. Well sir, Pennsy didn't even bother looking. She just moved in with me upstairs and folks hereabouts figgered I was some sort of Juan Casanova what with me having a dish like Pennsy to keepen me warm of nights.

She was terrible nice to me and I done the best I could by her and she might still be here iffen that Bannister feller hadn't up and bought her like she was a side of beef.

Well, I don't got me no complaints. She was sure a pleasure to have around and to boot I founden out that there little black mole on her fanny ain't no phoney iffen you know what I mean.

Jiggs Argyle looked downright forlorn.

He took out an old red bandana and wiped his eyes. He said, "You ever gitten a chancet, you be sure to tell Pennsy ole Jiggsy says howdy."

I said, "I'll do that."

Jiggs said, "Mister, you don't figger they gonna convict her, do you?"

I threw a ten-dollar bill on the bar and started for the door. I stopped and came back and put my hand on Jiggs Argyle's shoulder. I said, "Jiggs, there just ain't no way. If you know what I mean."

It was raining cats and cross-eyed dragons when I left the Stumble Out Inn.

be Golwitz.

Just about any old word-mechanic could have done a big book about Abe.

If he hadn't died laughing in the process.

Abe had been a shady legend around town for years. He was a purveyor of women. The female body has been a marketable commodity for some time so it wasn't that Abe had selected a barren field of endeavor. It was just that he went at it all wrong. Abe didn't put a few hustlers on street corners and split the take. Not Abe. That would have been much too simple. Abe approached the business with stealth and mind-boggling strategy. He was an innovator and he was to his chosen profession exactly what I have been to mine. A complete bust-out.

In the beginning there had been that home secretary thing. It was by considerably less than accident that Abe's first home secretary customers proved to be none other than vice-squad detectives Kurowski and Laird. When the home secretary arrived at the appointed place she wasted no time removing her clothing and throwing herself merrily into the sack. Vice-squad detectives Kurowski and Laird made polite inquiries as to the whereabouts of her typewriter. Almost without hesitation she replied, "Typewriter? What the hell typewriter?" and she was taken into custody on suspicion of being something other than a genuine home secretary.

That was when Abe got down to some serious innovating. In almost no time he came up with a gimmick called Dial-A-Cook. It didn't get off the ground. One hard-of-hearing old duffer failed to get the drift. He really wanted a home-cooked meal. The confused hooker did her best but she burned the house down while she was at it, and vice-squad detectives Kurowski and Laird escorted her to the nearest bastille.

Abe returned to the drawing board. He had learned something. Never dispatch poorly trained operatives. The girls of Abe's Let-A-Lovely-Lady-Sing-You-To-Sleep-Service knew "Rockabye Baby" by heart. It was a firm requirement. The second of the lullaby ladies didn't make it to the tree-top before down came the entire insane operation—Abe Golwitz and all.

Vice-squad detectives Kurowski and Laird again.

Abe stopped innovating. He took a lease on the Golden Garter on Wilson Avenue. Things didn't go much better. An irate stripper named Pennsylvania Woods stormed through the curtains completely nude and the Garter had been pad-locked for thirty days.

When Abe reopened he needed new dancers. One of these was a dark, slender, hollow-eyed young creature who read books about voodoo and would strip only to the "Funeral March" from *Gotterdammerung*. She insisted on being billed as Passionata Draculata. Abe chuckled good-naturedly. He chuckled good-naturedly until Passionata Draculata lunged into a capacity crowd and bit two customers.

Kurowski on the neck and Laird in the hindquarters.

Abe went legitimate. He opened a small nightspot on Cicero Avenue. He called it Abe's Place. For years Abe's Place muddled through without hint of sin, but in recent months it had been rumored that good-looking, highly cooper-ative ladies were frequenting the establishment, and that some of these had been known to depart the place with upward of a half-dozen escorts over the span of a single evening.

The cab dropped me off shortly after five. Abe's Place didn't open until six, but the doors were already ajar. This was a crafty maneuver dedicated to letting flies out and fresh air in, and it was every bit as effective as the rest of Abe's crafty maneuvers. I followed a reluctant sunbeam into cavernlike darkness swarming with a variety of insects and choked by the odors of stale beer, tobacco smoke, and ammonia. A burly, needle-nosed bartender stacked murky cocktail glasses on a leatherette-covered backbar, and an old black man hummed "Where Could I Go but to the Lord" while he sloshed a slimy mop over the broken tiles of the dance area.

I recognized Abe Golwitz from *Globe* photographs. He was a big, graying man with wire-framed glasses and a paunch that resembled a lopsided basketball. He wore a wrinkled tan gabardine suit and his flowered shirt was hopelessly wilted. He sat in a booth staring disconsolately at a sheet of typed figures.

I sat down across from him and said, "Abe, I'm Rip Deston of the *Globe.*"

Abe leaned back and exhaled loudly. He pushed his glasses high into his kinky graying hair. He said, "Sonofabitch, what's with you goddam reporters? If I open a hamburger stand, you rotten bastards figure I stole the ketchup."

I said, "Oh, not me, Abe. You open a hamburger stand and I run right home and count my cattle."

Abe folded his sheet of figures and pushed it to one side. He said, "Look, Deston, this is a kosher operation."

I winked at him, "That's what Hitler said about the Sudetenland."

Abe said, "Hitler, Shitler."

I said, "Abe, I'm not here to blast your two-bit cathouse. I just want to talk about Eloise Henderson."

Abe stared blankly.

I said, "You know, Abe. The little blonde knockout who put on her birthday suit that night at the Garter. The one who has her ass in a sling over the Bannister thing."

Abe sighed and grinned. The sigh was born of relief and the grin was of amused recollection.

Abe said, "Pennsy."

His voice fairly caressed the name.

I turned on my little tape recorder.

Oh, that Pennsy.

You know I really liked the chick. Honest to God, I did. Sure, she gave me some trouble and she was strictly a hands-off-the-merchandise type, but she was the only Garter gal I never nailed and she was the only one I ever really wanted. I used to lie awake nights thinking about her.

She wasn't cut out to be a stripper. Not Pennsy. Maybe that's why she was so damn good at it. She came across like the gal next door and lots of times what looked like too much rouge was a plain old country girl blush.

Took me a long time to peg her as the gal that's on trial downtown, because I don't remember her real name. It could have been Bertha Bellyblatt for all I know. At the Garter she was always Pennsy.

Hey, can you imagine a Bible-quoting stripper? Hell, that Pennsy knew the Bible better than the guys that wrote it. She had a Bible shot for damn near everything that happened. Like that night I went ass-over-tea kettles down the furnace room steps, and Pennsy said something about me falling into the ditch I had made. When I asked her what she meant by that, she told me to look it up in *Psalms*. Another time she called me an unclean and hateful bird. Boy, that broad hated my guts.

Funny part is I never did anything to her except try to speed up her act. She sure fixed my ass for that. Got me closed up for thirty days.

But, oh, sweet Jesus, what a glorious hunk of female! Bet I could get a couple hundred a session for her right now.

Roll it all up and I'll tell you about Pennsy.

Class, baby, strictly class!

Hell, Pennsy had more class by accident than most broads got on purpose.

I killed my tape recorder and stood up. I said, "Abe, thanks much."

Abe shrugged and said, "So it's nothing." He gave me a wink. "Could you handle a little action? Twenty or fifty?"

"I said, "No, thanks, Abe. Twenty's too young and I already got one fifty."

Abe shook his head. He said, "Price, dummy. Twenty for a quickie, and fifty for a party."

I shook my head.

Abe asked, "How do you think the trial will go?"

I said, "No sweat, Abe. The bum will win it in a walk."

Abe Golwitz came piling out of his booth like a bull elephant out of a cane brake. He shook his big fist under my nose. He yelled, "Hit the road, Junior! Pennsy is no bum!"

When I left Abe's Place, I noticed a plain black Ford sedan parked across the street.

I recognized its occupants.

Vice-squad detectives Kurowski and Laird.

That night I holed up in my Logan Square apartment with my little tape recorder, my typewriter, three packs of cigarettes, and a fifth of Clinch Mountain.

Clancy called. "All right, goddammit, I believe I have a right to know what's going on."

I said, "Nothing's going on."

Clancy said, "I haven't seen hide or hair of you in twenty-four hours."

I said, "I've been pretty busy."

Clancy said, "Don't give me that pretty busy crap. Who is she?"

I said, "Who?"

Clancy said, "Your new girl friend, that's who!"

I said, "Clancy, how the hell could I use a new girl friend? I got enough goddam problems with my old girl friend."

Clancy said, "What do you mean old, you sonofabitch?"

I said, "I didn't mean old like you think I meant old."

Clancy said, "Why, I can screw you to death!"

I said, "I think I noticed that back in '44."

Clancy hung up on me. I poured a drink and tried to remember a time when Clancy hadn't hung up on me. I couldn't.

I dialed my own number and shoved the receiver under a sofa cushion.

I stared into the amber depths of my Clinch Mountain and grinned from ear to ear. I had the dynamite to blow Eloise Henderson out of her quiet little shell.

She had stripped for the benefit of drunken slobs. She had shacked with a busted-down tavern keeper. She had moved in with Bannister on an arrangement that had less dignity than a ghetto garage sale.

Abe Golwitz had said she wasn't a bum. The hell she wasn't a bum. She was a bum without peer. She was worse than that. She was a murderous little hyena who had killed the man who had befriended both of us.

She went around with her guileless face and her sudden, sunny smile and she fired a few Biblical salvoes and she fooled everybody in sight.

Everybody but me.

I stayed up half the night to put it on paper. I wound it tight and headed it STRAPPED STRIPPER STRIKES GOLD.

Sam Cohen had gone to New York for a wedding. Norm

Harper was sitting in for him. Norm was up to his peaches in work. He let it roll through without a scratch.

It smoked up three columns of the Thursday morning *Globe.*

Page One.

t was Friday morning and I had an hour to kill before going to the courtroom. I was standing at the editorial room coffee machine with Ada Goldberg and Betty Anzivino. Ada Goldberg said, "That was some article, Ripper. It's a good thing for the Henderson girl that the jury won't get to see it."

Betty Anzivino said, "With all the newshounds in this town, it's a wonder somebody else didn't stumble onto the facts."

I said, "I got the door open by accident."

Ada said, "Sure, but the prosecution could have flushed the story if it had really been on the ball."

I said, "I don't know. Her past is pretty murky. She's out of Pennsylvania maybe. Her name is Eloise Henderson maybe. She was a stripper and a bit of a vagabond and where do we go from there?"

Betty said, "Well, if she'd been on any police blotters it would have surfaced by now."

I said, "I can tell you one thing. She doesn't have an enemy on earth or somebody would have been blowing whistles a long time ago."

Ada said, "If there were whistles to blow."

I said, "There you are."

Betty said, "Norm Harper was a little worried yesterday. He thinks maybe he should have read your article before instead of after. He's afraid Sam may get sore."

Ada said, "Oh, it'll be all right. Sam will see it in New York. If he doesn't like it he'll cool off by the time he gets back."

There was a low rumbling sound in the hall. Three-hundred-pound Sam Cohen came busting into the editorial room like a brahma bull into a Bohemian bakery. He was brandishing Thursday's *Globe* high over his head. Like a crazed Turk brandishes a scimitar. Sam's hair was standing straight up and his eyeballs were popping straight out. He was jumping around like his drawers were on fire and he waved his arms like a demented puppet.

He spewed an unbroken torrent of Yiddish and Italian.

I looked at the girls and shrugged. I said, "Translate, please."

Betty Anzivino said, "Well, first he is going to *farbrenen* Norm Harper at the *slup.*"

Ada Goldberg said, "That means he will burn him at the

stake and then he is going to *crocifiggere* the circulation manager."

Betty said, *"Crocifiggere* means 'crucify.' Abe promises to *shisn* all the janitors."

Ada said, "The translation of *shisn* is 'shoot.' For a grand finale he vows he will *castrare* Rip Deston."

I looked at Betty Anzivino. I said, "Does *castrare* mean what it sounds like it means?"

Betty lowered her eyes and nodded. She said, "Such a waste."

Sam saw me standing with Ada and Betty. He announced that Ada Goldberg and Betty Anzivino would be hanged.

I said, "Well, at least you're getting hanged in English."

Sam announced that they would be hanged from the flagpole.

I said, "More English, by God."

Sam announced that they would be hanged from the flagpole at dawn.

I said, "Still in English."

Sam announced that they would be hanged from the flagpole at dawn by the *pelatons.*

Ada said, "Oh, my God, what the hell does that mean?"

I said, "Honey, that was French and you have nothing to worry about."

Sam indicated that I should go into his office. He did this with a series of motions vaguely reminiscent of Warren Spahn's fast ball delivery. Except that Sam was right-handed.

I closed the door behind us and Sam slammed his Thursday *Globe* to the floor. He said, "Rip, I've changed my mind. I'm not going to castrate you."

I said, "Gee, thanks, Sam."

Sam said, "I am going to cut out your bleeping heart with my bleeping ballpoint pen!"

I said, "Sam, is something wrong?"

That did it.

Sam threw a three-foot rubber plant through the window. He threw a four-foot rubber plant through the window. He grabbed a six-foot rubber plant. He threw it through the window. He looked around. He pushed an intercom button. He said, "Suzanne, where the hell is my five-foot rubber plant?"

Suzanne said, "You threw it through the window last week."

Sam's voice was hoarse and quavering. He said, "Rip, you're writing dangerous and highly prejudiced material! You're convicting the Henderson broad before the bleeping jury even gets the bleeping case!"

I said, "Well, Jesus Christ, Sam, she's a goddam cold-blooded killer! For a few million bucks she shoved that nice old bastard straight into hell!"

Sam said, "If he was such a nice old bastard maybe he ain't in Hell. Maybe he's in Heaven where there ain't no drunk, washed-up baseball players running around making off like they are newspaper reporters!" Sam swept a vase of flowers from his desk. He said, "Why, you aren't reporting a bleeping trial, you're conducting a bleeping one goddam man bleeping venbleepingdetta!" He jumped up and down on his Thursday *Globe*. Dust spurted. He said, "This bleeping crap is largely unsubbleepingstantiated!"

I said, "Cool it, Sam. I didn't report it as largely substantiated crap. I reported it as crap I just happened to hear."

Sam said, "Well, goddammit, you can't bleep up my front page with crap you just happened to hear! Why, only yesterday I just happened to hear that the bleeping Martians had invaded bleeping Egypt!"

I said, "I just happened to hear that too, Sam, only I just happened to hear that they'd invaded bleeping Israel."

Sam said, "If this floozie gets off the hook she'll sue! She'll own this bleeping newspaper!"

I said, "If she gets off the hook she won't have to sue. She'll inherit the *Globe* flat out."

Sam turned pale. He said, "Oh, my God, that's right! Then she'll fire me for putting you on the goddam story."

I said, "Well, at least she might get that third-floor john fixed. Last week Edna Farksworth peed in her pants before she got to the second floor."

Sam dropped into his swivel chair and mumbled softly in Yiddish and Italian.

I said, "Look, Sam, if Eloise Henderson beats this rap, she won't sue anybody. She'll disappear. Hell, give *me* a few million bucks and *I'll* disappear."

Sam banged a foot on the floor. He said, "Well, by God, that's fair! How long do I get to raise the money?" He leaned back and lit an Italian stogie. He smiled at the thought.

The door opened. A copyboy stuck his head into the office. He said, "Hey, anybody in here want a rubber plant? Adams Street is full of them!"

Sam was wrong.
    Eloise Henderson didn't sue.
I was right.
She left town the day after she was acquitted.

The memories rode away on spectral steeds of cigarette smoke.

I sat on my chrome-plated, foam-rubber-padded, red Naugahyde-covered barstool. I rested my elbows on the wood-grained-formica-topped bar. I listened to tape-recorded swirling strings and flawless muted brass. Cool, precisely conditioned air caressed the back of my neck.

I looked around. Sheer-bloused brassiereless young women chatted with giggling, purse-carrying young men fresh from hairdressing salons.

It was just a dandy world.

Drugs and abortion were a way of life and homosexuality

73

was chic. Students waved enemy banners and burned American flags to the applause of the broadcasting industry. Public schools spent fortunes to teach Peruvian pottery-making and Indian basket-weaving to high school seniors who didn't know how to read or write. Television networks pumped raw sewage into adolescents and called it freedom of speech. Long hair, three guitar chords, and a steam-whistle voice could make you a millionaire in a week. Beautiful murderesses were freed ever so casually. God was deader than Martin Bannister, and the big city was coiled around my neck like a boa constrictor.

I thought of a trite expression. You can take the boy out of the country, but you can't take the country out of the boy.

When you're born in Saddleback Knob, Ohio, and raised in Cornelius, Ohio, you're a country boy.

Country boys have great advantages. Lonesome locomotive whistles and clear nights with big copper moons and fog on the dawn fields and dreamy summer afternoons. And silence. The great all-healing potion. If you aren't country, you don't know the first damn thing about silence.

Take a country boy out of the country. Bewilder him with two seasons of minor league baseball and blind him with three in the majors. Add a war, a bad leg wound, and six months in the hospital. Throw in nearly a quarter-century of big-city newspaper work. Surround him with drunks, pimps, whores, sex deviates, crooked politicians, fast buck artists, neon signs, polluted air, and contaminated water. Sprinkle with cheap women, drench in expensive whiskey, blend well, and you just have to wind up with a bone-weary bastard named Rip Deston.

But you still haven't taken the country out of the boy.

Mario was working the south end of the bar and he had been watching me. When he poured my next Clinch Mountain he asked, "You still got that Henderson dame on your mind?"

I answered, "More or less."

Mario said, "Don't let it bug you, Rip. Maybe she was really innocent."

I snorted, "If that little scorpion is innocent, Sam Cohen is a Nazi."

Mario said, "Don't let Sam Cohen hear you say that."

I said, "Screw Sam Cohen."

Mario grimaced. Under his breath he said, "Hold it, Rip, hold it!"

The barstool next to mine screeched in metallic agony as Sam Cohen hoisted his three hundred pounds aboard. Sam dragged a yellow silk handkerchief from a pocket of his gray sharkskin suit. He mopped his glistening brow. He said, "Rip, I want you should do me a favor." Sam had been raised in New York and sometimes he still talked that way.

I lit a cigarette and didn't say anything.

Sam continued, "I want you should find me a reason to fire you."

I said, "Shucks, nothing to it. I'm plastered during working hours."

Sam made an impatient gesture. "Aw, come on, Rip, I mean something that don't happen every damn day."

I shrugged, "Oh."

Sam asked, "Did you get over to that peace demonstration this morning?"

I answered, "Yeah, the peace demonstrators beat up seven cops and set fire to a supermarket."

Sam frowned. "Things are getting worse."

I said, "No, they're getting better. Last week they beat up fifteen cops and blew up an armory."

That was when Sam told me that I was going to Catastrophe, Missouri.

And *that* was why the third Thursday of May 1968 was memorable.

Sam began, "I just had a call from old Bert Clangingham at the *Catastrophe Clarion.*"

I nodded and said, "Oh, yes, good old Bert Clangingwho at the *Catastrophe Clariwhat.*"

Sam went on, "Clangingham founded the *Clarion* in 1925 and developed it into a solid money-maker. He loaned Bannister the down-stroke money to buy the *Globe* after it went bust during the depression. We still have a working agreement with the *Clarion.*"

I said, "By God, Sam, these tidings have reduced me to quivering jelly." I motioned to Mario. "Perhaps another Clinch Mountain will enable me to regain my customary rocklike composure." I downed my Clinch Mountain and regained my customary rocklike composure.

Sam watched me with facial expressions normally reserved for the witnessing of public executions by decapitation. He said, "Now, may I go on, goddammit?"

I said, "Oh, pray do."

Sam said, "Bert Clangingham thinks there's a story down there worthy of big-city readers' interest."

I came back, "Don't tell me some sonofabitch spiked the punch at the PTA meeting."

Sam said, "It's Catastrophe's Centennial."

I smirked, "Hot damn. I bet they got real live horses in the big parade."

Sam said, "What's more, a religious sect has purchased a piece of ground and it's building a tower." He put a match to an Italian stogie. "To Heaven."

I said, "Somebody already tried that. I think they blew it."

Sam said, "Yes, but we missed out on that one. Rip, think of all that small-town excitement. What a golden opportunity to do a homespun yarn that would twang the heartstrings of *Globe* subscribers. Not every reporter gets a shot at such a big dripping slice of Americana. Lord, just think of what Mark Twain would have done with it!"

I said, "Sam, there are a couple of drawbacks here and the first is that I ain't Mark Twain."

Sam said, "Aw, who cares?"

I answered, "Well, probably Mark Twain for one."

Sam asked, "Okay, what's the other drawback?"

I said, "I ain't going to Catastrophe, Missouri."

Sam said, "Look, Rip, this is right down your alley. You're from a hick town and you got a feeling for 'em. Run down there and soak up the local color. Shade-tree philosophers and village blacksmiths and the like. Just go where your heart leads you."

I smiled, "I've already done that, Sam. I've been here since the bar opened."

Sam said, "Think about all that cow manure and new-mown hay."

I said, "I think it's a bit early for new-mown hay." But I was considering it and it was beginning to appeal to me. I asked, "How do you get to Catastrophe, Missouri?"

Sam answered, "On the Little Thunder Custard Corners and Catastrophe Railroad."

I said, "Knock it off, Sam."

Sam said, "I'm leveling. You'll catch it out of Skinchburg at nine in the morning."

I asked, "Where is Skinchburg?"

Sam answered, "Sixty miles northeast of Custard Corners."

I said, "Skip it, Sam. Get yourself another boy."

Sam said, "Be ready at six. I'll have Moe Porter drive you out to Skinchburg." He smiled smugly. He slid from his barstool and it chirped with happy relief. He waddled out whistling "Poor Butterfly."

Or it might have been "Tiptoe Through the Tulips."

Sam couldn't carry a tune in a basket.

A trite expression.

I caught Mario's eye and made the Clinch Mountain sign.

A few drinks later I left money on the bar and went home. I set the alarm and flopped into bed and dreamed of quiet country roads. I dreamed of little white churches with tilted steeples and cracked bells and splintered pews and wheezing pump organs that played "What a Friend We Have in Jesus."

I dreamed of dragonflies in the sunshine and blackberry patches in the rain and creaking steps to sagging front porches, where old swings hung on rusty chains and dusty books from musty attics were read by country boys.

Country boys who left it all to play baseball.

On Friday morning my pillow was damp.

It had been a warm night.

Moe Porter was waiting in front of my apartment building in one of the *Globe*'s green Fords. I threw my stuff into the front seat and climbed into the back. I was asleep before we left the curb.

I came out of it at a dusty crossroads station where a weatherbeaten sign said SKINCHBURG. Moe said, "We had three detours since we left Chicago and we just made it. The train will be here in five minutes."

Two hours later the Little Thunder Custard Corners and Catastrophe Railroad Blue Bullet wobbled into Skinchburg. The Blue Bullet's only car was red. The rickety diesel engine was black, but it might have been blue if it had been washed. I waved so long to Moe and got on. I nodded to the conductor. He was a short, owlish man with a wart on his chin. I asked, "What happened?"

The conductor said, "If something happened, I never heard nothing about it."

I said, "You're two hours late."

The conductor drawled, "Oh, that ain't important. We can make up two hours between here and Custard Corners."

I asked, "It's sixty miles from here to Custard Corners, right?"

The conductor answered, "Right."

I said, "I think you better let me off."

The conductor said, "Ain't nothing to get all shook over. Usually takes four hours. If Joe can wind 'er up to thirty we'll make 'er in two." He thought about it. He said, "Providing we don't git derailed again."

I said, "Again?" I brushed sweat from my forehead. I said, "How often do you get derailed?"

The conductor mused, "Well, let's see now." He counted on his fingers. He said, "I don't think we got derailed last Monday."

I took a seat and dug into my suitcase for a bottle of Clinch Mountain.

I was the only passenger on the Never-Never Land Special.

The countryside crawled by. Rutted roads and tin mailboxes on crooked posts and milk cans on wooden platforms. Splintered barns and canted outhouses. Brown and white cows in rolling green fields and dusty pickup trucks and tiny grocery stores with Coca-Cola signs and gas pumps in front. An old man driving a tractor and a pig-tailed blonde girl in faded blue jeans on a plodding sway-backed chestnut mare. Gray pigeons on corncribs and sparrows on telephone wires and white ducks on ponds and crows in pin oak trees. Two tykes jumping up and down and waving. A spotted dog every half-mile barking in the time-honored tradition of spotted dogs the world over.

I got up and walked to the rear of the swaying car and watched the tracks recede into a never-ending V behind us. Back there somewhere was the kid who had left home with visions of becoming the greatest baseball star of all time. He became the first player to hit into five consecutive double plays. Back there was the soldier who had stormed ashore at New Georgia determined to win a Congressional Medal of Honor. He became the first casualty of the campaign and he never laid eyes on an enemy soldier. Back there was the busted-up war veteran who had taken a newspaper job with intentions of winning Pulitzer Prizes faster than they could be awarded. He became the hack who drank Clinch Mountain faster than it could be distilled.

Forty-nine years old and working on the backstretch to fifty.

Wasted years.

A nobody.

Too late now.

Well, what the hell.

If you can't lift it, paint it.

They used to say that in the army.

We rumbled through Fodderfield and Freetowne and Brownwater and New Hay City and Boltonbog and some others. The Clinch Mountain bottle was empty and I dozed as twilight stained the fields purple. I was awakened by a series of lurches and thumps and the conductor screaming, "Catastrophe! This is it! Catastrophe! End of the line! Everybody off! Catastrophe!" He really hadn't needed to carry on like that. He could have just mentioned it casually. What the hell, there were only the two of us.

It was nearly ten-thirty when I stepped from the aged railroad car into a clear, star-strewn night. The old diesel throbbed wearily away and I was alone in the darkness. I stood in the vast silence and looked in all directions. I heard gravel crunching. A giant of a man lumbered out of the gloom. Like Godzilla out of Tokyo Bay. His voice was about six octaves lower than October thunder. He boomed, "You Rip Deston?"

I said, "Yes, sir."

The big man squashed my hand in a paw the size of a country skillet. He said, "I'm Constable Westwood. Bert Clangingham said I should meet you."

I flexed my fingers and said, "Mighty nice of you."

Westwood picked up my suitcase and typewriter like you pluck bits of lint from your cuff. He said, "I seen you play ball oncet in '41. It was a doubleheader in New York and you hit into five straight double plays."

I said, "You must have missed the triple play."

Westwood said, "Yeah, I was in the washroom."

We walked to a Chevy pickup truck that had several bales of straw in its back end. By the dash lights I could see that Westwood was probably in his sixties. He was a gnarled man with silver at his temples and a great craggy jaw and eyes of blue slate. He was the sort of man young punks avoid if they entertain serious ideas of becoming middle-aged punks. He said, "Bert got you booked into Ma Stinson's boardinghouse. The hotel is full-up on account of the Centennial."

I said, "Right about now the nearest hayloft sounds good."

Westwood said, "Ma Stinson's is nice. Best damn cooking in town and telephones in all six rooms. Feather beds and country music on the radio from dawn to midnight."

We rolled down the main drag of Catastrophe, Missouri. Two establishments showed lights. The Catastrophe Hotel and a saloon with a sign that said BEER AND WINE NO

HARD STUFF. I said, "What's this I hear about some religious tower?"

Westwood's laugh was deep and mellow. He said, "Oh, that's them First Church of Almighty God Our Savior and Redeemer folks. Back last winter they bought a roadside patch of land from Si Willow. They been trying to build a tower to Heaven since March. Damn thing keeps falling down."

I said, "Well, why don't they just wait? They're all going to Heaven anyway."

Westwood said, "Yeah, but they're in a big hurry. Reverend Dawson had a vision that said they got to be through by Labor Day."

I said, "Apparently Heaven has the same holidays we have."

Westwood said, "They got 'er back up to fifteen foot again and they do seven maybe eight foot a day."

I said, "At that rate they won't even be out of sight by Labor Day."

Westwood said, "Yeah, Reverend Dawson says he got to take that up with God shortly."

We pulled up in front of a rambling gray frame house and Westwood led me in without knocking. A small, gray-haired lady met us in the parlor. She wore a blue gingham dress and she carried the biggest white cat I've ever seen. She smiled a chipped-dentures smile and said, "Mr. Deston, you'll be in the first room at the top of the stairs."

I nodded and grabbed my things.

She said, "Would you care for a cup of coffee?"

I said, "Not tonight, thanks."

She took the Constable's hand and said, "You'll stay, won't you, Chet?"

Westwood said, "Can't think of no reason why not."

I waved to Westwood and said, "Thanks, Constable."

Westwood said, "Anytime at all."

Ma Stinson said, "Breakfast's at eight, dinner's at noon, and supper's at six. You'll hear the bell."

I nodded and started up the stairs.

Supper.

It had been a long time since I'd heard the word.

reakfast was served on Ma Stinson's sunporch at a great oval table covered with a blue and white checked cloth the size of a circus tent. I sat directly across from Kelly Clark, a ferret-faced little guy in a wild-colored plaid suit and a screaming-yellow shirt. Kelly Clark ate mechanically, rarely taking his eyes from the Racing Form near his coffee cup.

Next to Kelly Clark was a short, fat man whose shoulder holster was clearly visible. Ma Stinson introduced him as Stars And Stripes Forever Fogarty. On the back of Fogarty's left hand was a tattoo that said KILL JAPS. On the back of his right hand was a tattoo that said KILL MORE JAPS.

I asked, "Were you in the war?"

Stars And Stripes Forever Fogarty answered, "Yes, and I still am."

I said, "Oh?"

Stars And Stripes Forever Fogarty said, "They ain't through yet."

I said, "Is that right?"

Stars And Stripes Forever Fogarty said, "They got one great big hairy all-out banzai attack left in 'em and it could come any time now." He thumped his shoulder holster. He said, "We got to be ready."

On my right was a small, slender man with wild black hair. His eyes were gray and they glittered. He carried a Bible and he had insisted on saying grace before we ate. Before the ritual was complete the eggs were nearly cold. His name was Lester Critchlow and he told me that he was beyond doubt the world's greatest Bible authority. He said, "Anything you want to know about the Bible you just ask."

I said, "Okay."

To my left was a large, bald, bulldog-faced man named Nate Jones. Nate Jones was in his late fifties and he had melancholy eyes. He told me that he worked afternoons at the railroad roundhouse, that his life was empty, that nothing happened before he went to work, and that everybody was in bed by the time he got back. He told me that he was sick and tired of just waiting for something to happen.

I said, "Oh, I'm sure something will happen one of these days."

Nate Jones scowled ominously. He said, "You're goddam right something will happen one of these days!"

I watched a willowy brunette come onto the sunporch. She was built the way women should be built and she walked the way they should walk, shoulders back and free-striding. She wore a simple black-on-white print dress and three-inch heeled white pumps. She carried a white handbag and she had on a huge pair of sunglasses, the kind that obscure half your face. She flicked an inquisitive glance at me and sat to take one flapjack and a cup of black coffee.

Lester Critchlow was talking to Kelly Clark. He said, "Dawson is a fool. He'll never make it to Heaven on no ole wood tower. They got to use brick and mortar like them people when they built the Tower of Babel."

I said, "Where did they build that Tower of Babel, anyway?"

Critchlow said, "Why, in Babylon, of course."

The brunette opened her white handbag and took out a small leather notebook and a gold-plated ballpoint pen. She wrote something on a page and tore it out and folded it. She finished her snack and rose gracefully to her feet. As she left the room she placed the folded paper at my elbow. I opened it. The handwriting was beautiful. It said, "The Tower of Babel was erected on a plain in the land of Shinar and it was probably no more than seven stories high." The note was signed "H.C."

I slipped it into my shirt pocket and said, "Does that lady live here?"

Critchlow said, "Yeah. Her name is Cornstalk or something and I think she's hooked up with the newspaper."

Constable Westwood came in carrying a steaming mug of coffee. He clapped an enormous hand on my shoulder and said, "You want to see the Tower to Heaven?"

I checked for broken bones and found none. I said, "That's one reason I'm here."

Critchlow snorted. He said, "You better hurry. It's about due to fall down again. Brick and mortar! Brick and mortar is the only answer!"

Westwood and I stepped into a sunny Saturday morning and drove west in his pickup truck. Westwood said, "You probly ain't gonna believe what you see out there. The whole business is cuckoo."

I said, "Well, as long as they keep on doing what they're doing, you won't have to worry about them doing anything else."

Westwood said, "You got a point there."

We pulled into a corner of a heavily wooded tract on the edge of town. It was busier than an anthill. Men felled trees and dragged them into a clearing. Teenagers hacked the branches off. Women prepared food in big pots over log fires. They sharpened tools on old grindstones. They sang songs and clapped their hands like college cheerleaders. The tower jutted some twenty feet into the air. It was a crude structure that listed noticeably to starboard. There was a big sign nailed to its base. FIRST CHURCH OF ALMIGHTY GOD OUR SAVIOR AND REDEEMER OFFICIAL TOWER TO HEAVEN REVEREND RALPH J. DAWSON BUILDING SUPERINTENDENT ALSO CHIEF ARCHITECT GLORY HALLELUJAH PRAISE THE LORD AMEN.

I said, "Funny, I don't hear any chain saws."

Westwood said, "Chain saws ain't allowed. It all got to be done by hand like Noah built the ark."

I said, "Why?"

Westwood said, "Only Dawson and God knows."

We left the pickup truck and walked to the foot of the

tower where a gaunt, skull-faced man in a threadbare black suit urged his workers to greater efforts by intoning, "All right, children, let's hit it for Jesus!"

Westwood smiled. He said, "Hey, Rev, be sure you don't damage them pearly gates."

Reverend Dawson looked up with feverish eyes. In a sepulchral voice he said, "Oh, there ain't no danger of that." He hauled out a huge piece of paper and unfolded it.

Westwood said, "What's that?"

Dawson said, "It's my map of Heaven."

Westwood gave me a nudge and a wink. He said, "That's right. I forgot about that map."

Dawson said, "You see, the pearly gates is right there." He stabbed the map with his forefinger. He slid the finger several inches to his right. He said, "We figger to enter the Holy City over here."

Westwood looked horrified. He said, "You gonna *sneak* in?"

Dawson laughed. A trifle wildly. He said, "We just want it to be a surprise. Can't you just see the expression on God's face when we come in the back way?" He slapped his knee and doubled up with laughter. He shouted, "Oh, glory, brother!"

Westwood said, "Listen, Rev, you better back off a few paces. If this thing falls over again you're liable to get to Heaven ahead of schedule."

Lester Critchlow approached, his Bible under his arm. Dawson saw him coming and whipped out his own Bible. They squared off. Dawson said, "I thought I told you to stay out of here."

Critchlow said, "I'm trying to be helpful! You're off on the wrong foot. They used brick and mortar on the Tower of Babel."

Dawson said, "Yeah, but you'll notice they didn't get to Heaven on it."

Critchlow said, "Well, that was only on account of nobody knowed what the other feller was talking about. You people can't do it on a wood tower."

Dawson said, "Well, I just happened to of had me a vision what said we can."

Critchlow said, "Oh, that was only a ole ordinary Class B vision you had."

Dawson said, "It was a Class A vision. I know a Class A vision when I see one. It was in color with sound and everything."

Critchlow said, "You're simply gonna have to use brick and mortar!"

Dawson said, "Brick and mortar is man-made!"

Critchlow said, "So is hammers and nails!"

Westwood guided me toward his pickup truck. He said, "It happens every damn day. Critchlow is a Bible nut from over in Gopher Center. The minute he heard about this tower he come busting in here talking about brick and mortar and he been talking about brick and mortar ever since."

We got into the pickup truck just as the tower groaned and came down with an earth-shaking crash. Timbers flew in all directions. Women screamed and men broke down and wept.

We pulled away as Critchlow waved his Bible in Dawson's face and Dawson hit Critchlow over the head with his. Westwood shook his head. He said, "Somebody's gonna get hurt out here and I got no legal way of stopping 'em." He sighed.

He said, "Ain't but four things can make a complete fool of a man."

I said, "Five."

Westwood said, "Women, baseball, politics, and religion. What else?"

I said, "Whiskey."

Westwood said, "By God, that's right." He pulled the pickup truck onto the shoulder and stopped.

He said, "Hand me that bottle out of the dash compartment."

It was ten ayem when Westwood dropped me in front of the tavern where the sign said BEER AND WINE NO HARD STUFF. It was a broken-down joint filled with locals wearing Stetsons, swilling beer, and talking about crops, cattle, and the Centennial celebration. I took a stool that afforded me a clear view of Main Street and I ordered a bottle of Old Washensachs. The barkeep said, "The big parade gonna be coming by in a few minutes. You got a real good seat fer it."

I said, "They gonna have horses?"

The barkeep said, "Oh, sure, lots of horses and the high-school band and the VFW and everything."

I said, "Wow."

The barkeep said, "The Centennial dance gonna be tonight at the high-school gym. You going?"

I said, "Do I need an invitation?"

The barkeep grinned. He said, "Shucks, no. Just walk in and start dancing."

I said, "Yeah, but with who?"

The barkeep said, "Hey, you oughta try that filly what works fer ole Bert Clangingham. She ain't got nobody last I heard." He looked me over. He said, " 'Course, you're just a mite old fer her."

I said, "What's her name?"

The barkeep shrugged. He said, "Hell, I dunno. Holly something-or-other, I think." He brought my beer. He said, "Watched you come in. Where'd you git that bum leg?"

I said, "The war."

The barkeep asked, "You limp that bad all the time?"

I answered, "Only when I walk."

The barkeep advised, "Maybe you better keep off that dance floor. They got them New Hay City Barnburners playing tonight and I mean they really git it on!"

I was on my fourth Old Washensachs when I heard the drums begin to thump. The Catastrophe Missouri Centennial parade came down Main Street.

There was an eighteen-piece band garbed in red and yellow. It was playing what may have been the "National Emblem March," but would have passed for the "Ride of the Valkyries" in the concert hall of Valhalla. There were twenty-some guys wearing VFW overseas caps. Most were in their late forties and all were out of step. The Catastrophe fire engine came next followed by the town ambulance. Their sirens wailed in hellish harmony. There was a float towed by Constable Westwood's Chevy pickup truck. It sported dozens of red and yellow paper roses and a well-endowed young damsel who waved a banner that said HAPPY ONE HUN- NERTH BRITHDAY CATASTROPHE MISSOURI. After the float came a large group of men on horses. They waved their Stetson hats and they yelled yippee and wahoo and whoopee and yahoo and a great many other ridiculous things and a horse kicked a popcorn vendor where it hurts like you can just hardly imagine. The popcorn vendor was quick to indicate that he needed help. He accomplished this by throw- ing himself heavily to the ground, clutching his groin, turn- ing pastel green and rolling like a barrel in a great many directions.

Word was sent to the ambulance driver whose frantic at- tempts to leave the parade resulted in a collision with the Ca- tastrophe fire engine and the two vehicles sat hopelessly locked together on Main Street.

When the big Centennial parade had turned the corner into history the barkeep strolled over with a fresh Old Washen- sachs. He said, "Say, I bet you ain't never seen no parade like that afore."

I said, "Well, not recently at any rate."

The barkeep looked through the window and said, "Hey, that's her!"

I said, "That's who?"

The barkeep said, "The young lady I was telling you about. The one in the black and white dress over there talking to ole Bert Clangingham."

The lady of the breakfast table sat on a bench in front of Jason's Dry Goods Store. Her absolutely perfect long legs were crossed. Her white handbag was perched in the lap of her simple print dress. She tapped absent-mindedly at a pendant earring. The breeze toyed daintily with wisps of her soft dark hair. Sunlight flamed on her enormous glasses. A white pump dangled precariously from the toes of a dainty foot. A lanky, hawk-faced man sat beside her. He was very, very old. He wore a green suit and an open-collared beige shirt. As they chatted she punctuated their conversation with sudden, bright smiles that vanished as quickly as they came. Her hands shifted slightly on her purse and I watched for the sparkle of sunlight on metal. No rings.

She was more than twenty years my junior but dirty old newspaper reporters can't help thinking.

I watched her stand to tell the old man goodbye and when she walked away my eyes were glued to her.

I knew nothing about her.

Except that no virgin had ever walked like that.

And never would.

ollowing my second piece of Ma Stinson's apple pie with honey, I went up to my room. I sat there until three in the afternoon, nipping at a bottle of Clinch Mountain, smoking like a volcano, poking at my typewriter, and cussing up a storm. I tried first person, second person, third person, and all three tenses. Nothing worked. There was something elusive about Catastrophe, Missouri, and I just couldn't nail it down. I did six pages, tore them up, and went down to the front porch.

I sat on a dilapidated old glider in the lazy, warm May afternoon and at some point in all that country silence I fell asleep.

I awakened to the certain knowledge that I was not alone. Hyacinth perfume doesn't come from nowhere.

She was sitting beside me on the glider.

I said, "Was I snoring?"

She said, "No."

Just one word of a single syllable, but it gave me goose-bumps.

I said, "I must have been tired."

She asked, "Did I startle you?"

I answered, "Not at all." My heart was trying to blow a hole in my chest, but not because I'd been startled.

She said, "You're Mr. Deston of the *Chicago Globe*."

I said, "And you're Holly Cornstalk."

She gave me a lightning-quick smile. She said, "Comstock, if you will."

I said, "Thanks for the word on the Tower of Babel." I offered her a cigarette and she took it. I held a match for her. My God, she was beautiful. She had big, round dark eyes and a flawless pert nose and a rose-petal mouth and a clean-cut jaw line that was firm without a trace of obstinacy.

Holly Comstock asked, "Will you be going to the dance this evening?"

I answered, "I suppose so. I'm down here to absorb as much local color as possible. I'm absorbing it, but I can't seem to get it on paper."

Holly gave me a fast, encouraging smile. She said, "It'll come. I've read some of your stuff and you're very good." She knocked her cigarette ash over the porch banister. "In rather blunt fashion, I might add." Her friendly wink removed any sting from the remark.

I asked, "Will you be at the dance?"

Holly answered, "Yes, I'm one of its official greeters."

I said, "Good, maybe I'll write about you."

Holly made a wry little face. She dropped her cigarette to the porch deck and ground it slowly under her foot. She said, "I hope you'll say something nice."

I said, "That shouldn't be difficult."

Holly stood and said, "Do you dance?"

I said, "I have a bad leg. Fast numbers give me trouble. Songs like 'Pennsylvania Polka,' for instance."

Holly stood and put out her hand and I took it without getting to my feet. It was warm, soft, and very smooth. Certainly not a hand that was accustomed to manual labor. I held it for a moment. She said, "Perhaps something slower? 'Beautiful Ohio'?"

I said, "I'll take a shot at it."

She nodded, gave me a brief smile, and went into the house. My hand was slightly cut from where her fingernails had dug in.

I sat on the old glider watching twilight close in on Catastrophe, Missouri, much as I had once sat on an old porch swing and watched it close in on Cornelius, Ohio. Twilight was my favorite time of day.

With some twilights came Susie Weatherby and this was one of them.

In my own clumsy, backhanded way, I had loved Susie, and I suppose I would have proposed to her if she hadn't proposed to me first. And twenty times daily after that. A man hates to be run down like a rabbit. Getting out of Cornelius had been easy. Getting back had been out of the question. You just don't hit the panic button and walk out on a woman the way I had walked out on Susie.

I tried to imagine the Susie of today but I couldn't find the handle. I figured she had married a solid-citizen type, the kind that never touches a drop, mows the lawn every Saturday morning, and goes to church twice on Sunday. He had probably driven her to sewing circle meetings on Thursday evenings and sat in Walt Disney movies with the kids until time to pick her up. I guessed that she had borne four children. That would make her a grandmother. What kind of grandmother? A scrawny, nervous, pecky grandmother or the fat, placid, giggling type? I could visualize neither. I saw only a slim, laughing girl with cornsilk hair and cornflower blue eyes, and I remembered her frantic, all-out way of making love and the utterly ridiculous things she would say while doing it. I remembered the way I would blow into her ear while she lay snuggled close to me afterward and how she would jump and threaten to kill me for it.

One thing I was sure of. Susie had starched her solid-citizen husband's shirt collars until the poor bastard's neck was raw. He'd be needing a tourniquet if he didn't choke to death first.

I had more than my share of regrets, but hurting Susie was the granddaddy of them all.

Susie hadn't deserved that kind of treatment.

Not for loving me the way she had.

I followed the buzzing, light-hearted crowds to the Catastrophe, Missouri High School gymnasium. It was located just three blocks south of Ma Stinson's boardinghouse. A number of young ladies waited inside the door. They wore corsages and they shook hands with all arrivals. Holly Comstock spotted me and came right over. She was a picture in her form-fitting black satin dress. Her hyacinth perfume double-clutched my heart. She took my hand and gave me a sudden, brilliant smile. She said, "Mr. Deston, I've already requested 'Beautiful Ohio'."

I said, "I got a feeling you'll regret that."

Holly gave me an encore smile and said, "No, I won't. Not for a moment. I'll be with you when the guests are in."

I found the bar and ordered a Clinch Mountain and water. Constable Westwood stopped by and slapped me on the back. I grabbed the edge of the bar and blinked until the room stopped revolving.

Westwood said, "Well, they got the new tower up to ten foot this afternoon. You want to go out again in the morning?"

I said, "It's the only game in town. I'd like to get a look at Dawson's map of Heaven."

Westwood chuckled. He said, "I wouldn't bother if I was you. Ain't nothing but a bunch of mumbo-jumbo Dawson claims he seen in a vision. Like Peter lives across the street from Paul and Josiah got a manna stand next door to John the Baptist's house."

I said, "Damn shame about that accident during the parade. The ambulance driver must have been embarrassed."

Westwood said, "Yeah, but he'd of been a lot more embarrassed if the Joe Gates Feed Emporium had caught fire along about that time."

I said, "How's that?"

Westwood said, "Joe Gates was driving the ambulance."

The New Hay City Barnburners struck up a lively ditty and the gym floor filled with couples. Westwood excused himself and made a beeline for Ma Stinson. They swung onto the floor like a pair of teenagers. I didn't know if they were lovers but it was obvious that they were very good friends.

I found a table and sat to watch the dancers. They whirled to "San Antonio Rose" and "Under the Double Eagle" and "Bring It on Down to My House, Honey." There was great happiness in the air and I owned a piece of it. I didn't miss Chicago thirteen cents' worth.

The dancing went on and on. Apparently the New Hay City Barnburners didn't take breaks and the residents of Catastrophe, Missouri, didn't need any.

I heard "When My Blue Moon Turns to Gold Again" and "Ain't Nobody's Business What I Do" and "Nine Pound Hammer." Then Holly Comstock was standing beside me. She said, " 'Beautiful Ohio' is next. Are you ready?"

I said, "Ready as I'll ever be." I stood and she stepped into my arms. Holly Comstock didn't dance, she floated. I committed twenty errors but she made me look good. She had the grace, the instincts, and the reflexes of a kitten. When the music stopped we were alone on the floor. There was a loud burst of applause. I looked around and said, "What's going on?"

Holly squeezed my arm and said, "Smile and wave, for God's sake! They're applauding us!"

She accompanied me back to the table and said, "I'll get drinks." When she returned with mine she said, "Clinch Mountain and water."

I said, "ESP?"

Holly said, "No. Word gets around."

I asked, "Holly, have you ever danced professionally?"

Holly sat across from me with a mischievous smile. She answered, "Just a few command performances at Buckingham Palace and the like."

I said, "I'm serious."

Holly waited while I held a match for our cigarettes. She sidestepped the query and said, "You covered Eloise Henderson's murder trial for the *Chicago Globe*." It was a statement, not a question. She said, "You really laid the wood to her."

I held Holly's eyes with mine. I said, "I certainly tried. She was guilty."

Holly frowned a perplexed little-girl frown. She asked, "How can you be certain of that?"

I said, "I have excellent radar."

Holly said, "Phooey."

I said, "You'd be surprised."

Holly said, "I still read your series on that trial. I have it in a scrapbook, every word. I was particularly impressed by your 'Strapped Stripper Strikes Gold' thing."

I said, "I'm delighted to hear that."

Holly said, "Do you realize that if the jury had seen that stuff, an innocent woman might have gone to prison for life?"

I said, "An innocent woman wasn't on trial."

Holly said, "You seemed to have lost sight of the fact that they were trying a woman for first-degree murder, not for the human mistakes she'd made."

I said, "Isn't murder a human mistake?"

Holly stood. She looked down at me with narrowed brown eyes. She said, "My room is at the north end of the hall. Will you come there tonight? I want to have a long talk with you."

I winked at her. I said, "I had a hunch on that."

Holly gave me a quick smile and turned it off. She winked back. She said, "Losers play hunches, Rip."

It was the first time she'd called me Rip.

I liked it.

I walked the long, narrow rug in Ma Stinson's squeaking midnight hallway. I tapped gently on the north-end door. In a moment it was opened by a breathtakingly beautiful blue-eyed woman with short honey-blonde hair. Through a sheer, light-blue robe a table lamp revealed the outlines of a body perfectly suited to a woman who would remove her clothing for money.

The woman searched my face for traces of surprise. She saw none. She said, "Come in, Rip."

I sat on a small couch behind a flimsy serving table on which I saw a bottle of Clinch Mountain, a pitcher of water, and two glasses. She said, "Sorry, no ice."

I poured a drink and said, "Jiggs Argyle said to tell you howdy."

Eloise Henderson sat beside me. She nodded and smiled her patented brief smile. She lit a cigarette and said, "Jiggsy. What a fine little man." She mixed a drink for herself and said, "How long have you known?"

I said, "I suppose there was something familiar about you all along, but I was never near you in the courtroom so the wig and tinted contact lenses and those big sunglasses threw me off. When you spoke to me this afternoon I knew for certain. I'd recognize your voice anywhere."

Eloise Henderson said, "I hope that's a compliment."

I said, "It is. You have a marvelous voice, Miss Henderson. Or should I call you 'Pennsylvania Woods'?"

A corner of her soft mouth twitched. She said, "Why don't you pretend you're my friend and call me 'Pennsy'?"

I lit a cigarette and said nothing.

She nipped at her drink and said, "I've been dying to meet you. I influenced Clangingham to bring you down here. I simply had to learn what sort of person would embark on the crackpot crusade you took up against me."

I said, "Why, Pennsy, I'm no crackpot. I'm just a law-abiding old country boy who frowns on murder."

Pennsy said, "A country boy with a nasty little chip on his shoulder."

I said, "Not me!"

Pennsy dropped her hand to her leg with an exasperated slapping sound. She said, "Yes, oh, yes! Tell me how you developed this hatred and why. I just have to know, dammit!"

I said, "Martin Bannister was my friend. Does that help?"

Pennsy put her hands to her face and laughed. It was a

musical laugh. Like distant wind-chimes. She said, "Oh, my God, my God!"

I said, "Is that funny?"

Pennsy said, "Rip, you've been barking up the wrong tree. There are two things that you should know about Marty Bannister. Are you interested?"

I said, "That's a damn fool question."

Pennsy turned and looked me full in the face. She said, "Marty Bannister was a suicide."

I shook my head. I said, "No way. Not Bannister."

Pennsy said, "Look back, will you? He took a vacation, remember?"

I said, "Of course I remember. He wasn't worth a damn when he came back."

Pennsy said, "Right, and do you know why? Because during that vacation he learned that he had leukemia."

I thought that one over. I said, "So he splattered himself all over a concrete patio instead of taking a nice quiet overdose of sleeping pills? I don't think so."

Pennsy ran a hand through her short honey-blonde hair. She said, "Rip, you knew Marty. He was the flamboyant, sudden sort. With Marty it had to be quick. He'd been leaning to suicide for months. We argued over the matter constantly. Even as late as ten minutes before he jumped."

I said, "I can't buy it."

Pennsy said, "You can't buy it because you haven't fought leukemia for seven years. Good God, you have no idea what he went through! He had just a short time remaining and it promised to be terrible. He was a physical wreck with nothing in his future but death. Try to put yourself in that position."

I said, "Leukemia was never mentioned."

Pennsy said, "Of course not, but just pick up a telephone and call Dr. Felix Schnickenfish at 202 North Michigan Avenue in Chicago. He has my permission to give you the facts."

I said, "If Bannister had leukemia and committed suicide why did you sweat out a murder trial?"

Pennsy said, "Stuart Richmond felt that Marty's name deserved better than a suicide footnote and I agreed. Also there were insurance provisions against suicide. From a strictly financial point of view, it was imperative that Marty's death go into the books as accidental. And, of course, Richmond didn't believe they'd indict me."

I said, "Richmond's more lawyer than prophet."

Pennsy laughed a quick, dry laugh. She said, "Yes, but we went the route to save the inheritance of a certain party. Richmond told me that if it began to get sticky, he'd throw in the towel and pull me out. Fortunately it didn't come to that."

I said, "It must have been an ordeal."

Pennsy said, "Rip, I had the liver scared out of me."

I said, "You looked cooler than a sunrise cucumber."

Pennsy said, "We have our facades and I'm no exception."

I rolled it around in my mind. She couldn't be bluffing. I could call Dr. Schnickenfish for two dollars. I sucked on my cigarette and tried to blow a smoke-ring. It came out lopsided. A fine symbol of my recent thinking.

Pennsy said, "I'd really appreciate it if you'd verify what I've told you."

I said, "You mentioned another thing I should know."

Pennsy put her hand on mine. I caught the faint scent of her hyacinth perfume. She looked at me with sadness in her blue eyes and she spoke with a slight catch in her voice.

She said, "Rip, Marty Bannister was your father."

The small room became smaller and the design of the faded wallpaper rushed at me like a runaway locomotive. My head roared like Niagara Falls. I sat without speaking. I mumbled something. It must have been a question because Pennsy was saying, "Look, Rip, I don't read tea leaves and I don't know the entire story, but during World War I Marty put in some time at Camp Sherman, Ohio, and your mother lived in neighboring Saddleback Knob. Her name was Rebecca."

I went back to that first afternoon at Angelo's. A backwoods army camp, Bannister had said. A backwoods army camp and a beautiful girl. In a flat voice I said, "Rebecca what?"

Pennsy put on her perplexed little-girl frown. She said, "Ashwell, I think. Something like that."

I said, "Lashwell."

Pennsy's frown cleared. She said, "That's right."

I said, "Look, goddammit, my father's name was Captain Raymond Deston and I've seen pictures of him. I've seen a marriage certificate, my birth certificate, and a half-dozen other documents."

Pennsy shook her lovely head. She said, "You've seen false documents thoughtfully provided by Marty to protect your mother's good name. Those photographs were of an old army buddy of Marty's."

I hadn't drowned yet but I was going down fast. I said, "My father was killed at Meuse-Argonne. My mother and I lived from his early investments."

Pennsy said, "Marty supported your mother until she died in 1940. Marty was a decent man and he never failed to meet his obligations."

I didn't clock the ensuing silence but it was one long sonofabitch.

I said, "What was your relationship with Bannister?"

Pennsy said, "Certainly far from what some people assumed it was. Marty was a dying man who asked me to see him through the hard going. In return he promised to remember me in his will. I was never his plaything. Men preoccupied with death aren't interested in sex, believe me."

I had come into the room armed to the teeth and prepared to reduce Eloise Henderson to confetti. Now I cowered like a whipped mongrel puppy. My world looked like Hiroshima after the bomb. Pennsylvania Woods wasn't the woman I had set out to destroy, I was the bastard son of a newspaper magnate, my mother had been Bannister's weekend party girl, and the man whose name I carried had never existed. My God, if it developed that Sam Cohen was a relative, I'd blow my brains out.

Pennsy was saying, "I met Marty at a social affair years ago. We chatted while the others danced. He said that it was a rare pleasure to meet an intelligent woman. After that we talked on the phone occasionally, but I never saw him again until he had learned of his affliction. He made his proposition and I accepted. I learned to love Marty in a very special way because he was a very special man. He was as good as his word. His will hasn't been completely ironed out, but I can tell you that I'm about to own fifty-one percent of the *Chicago Globe*."

I said, "Who gets the rest?"

Pennsy said, "Bert Clangingham. Clangingham gave Marty his start and Marty remembered that. It's an interlocking arrangement geared in a fashion that prevents either of us from selling until one owns it all. If I drop dead Clangingham gets my share and vice versa."

I said, "Well, you'll outlive Clangingham."

Pennsy said, "Good Lord, I hope so. He has more than fifty years on me." She made new drinks for us and said, "Rip, it was your inheritance that we fought to save. Six hundred thousand dollars of insurance money that now becomes a trust fund paying you twenty-five thousand a year when you retire from the *Globe*."

I swallowed hard. I croaked, "Good. I just retired. I can't handle this damn story anyway."

Pennsy shrugged. She said, "All right, put it in writing and I'll send it in, but I want you to understand that you couldn't have been fired. That's a firm provision in Marty's will. If you burn the building down they can't touch you."

I said, "There's a thought. How are you set for matches?"

Pennsy said, "Be serious."

I said, "I'm completely serious. I'll type the damn resignation tomorrow."

We sat quietly.

I wondered why I hadn't sensed something twenty-seven years earlier. I added up Bannister's unwarranted admiration, his job offers, his many kindnesses, and his blue jays.

And I had persecuted the innocent woman who had seen my dying father through his final days and gone through hell to preserve my inheritance.

Once a horse's ass always a horse's ass.

Pennsy sat watching me. She toyed with an end of the braided blue belt that kept her sheer robe closed tightly.

I said, "Why the hell didn't he tell me?"

Pennsy said, "He was afraid you'd turn your back and that would have broken his heart. He loved you so much, Rip. You'll never know how much."

I said, "He must have loved me, but I'll never understand why."

Pennsy said, "You're an admirable man. You've inherited Marty's decent streak. You've made mistakes but they were honest mistakes."

I said, "Jesus Christ, how blind can one man be?" I buried my face in my hands.

In a few minutes Pennsy said, "I wouldn't give a penny for a man who couldn't cry."

She waited and when I had stopped, she dried my eyes with a tiny hyacinth-scented hankerchief. She said, "Rip, this is for you." She pressed an end of her braided blue belt into my hand.

I looked at it. I said, "What the hell am I supposed to do with this rope?"

Pennsy said, "Oh, it's ever so simple. Just pull."

I glanced up from the belt end. Pennsy's blue eyes danced with challenge. I said, "You don't mean that."

Pennsy said, "I don't bluff."

I shook my head in disbelief. I said, "Look, I'm pushing fifty. In your book I have to be a very old man."

Pennsy said, "Rip, will you please pull the darned belt?"

I pulled the belt.

Slowly.

I saw its shoe-string bow come apart. I watched the sheer light-blue robe fall open. I said, "No, you don't bluff."

Pennsy said, "I don't have to bluff. I'm a lot of woman."

I said, "I can see that."

Sometime during that magic night Pennsy kissed me. She said, "Rip, was Saddleback Knob a nice little town?"

I said, "I don't remember it. We moved north when I was less than a year old."

Pennsy said nothing.

I said, "Now I know why. Bastard kids weren't well accepted in those days."

Constable Westwood was silent during our drive to the tower site. He could sense that I was in no mood for idle chatter and an exchange of good mornings had been the extent of our conversation.

She had made love like she danced, anticipating my every move, making my weaknesses strong and my strengths magnificent, meeting my unskilled thrusts with a wonderful hot wetness, gently but firmly, clinging to me as though I were a solitary straw on boundless waters, lightly but tightly, in full command all the way, making delicious little hungry sounds, teasing me, coaxing me to the brink, changing tempo to lead me again and again up the dark, lush hill, then mercifully

destroying me with breathtaking, blinding suddenness, waiting under me, stroking me until my breathing had slowed,
rolling me softly to my side, kissing me, telling me to sleep.

No inexperienced woman devours a man in that fashion.
Such prowess requires more than raw instinct. It had been as
much art as animal, but there had been nothing mechanical
about those deep, bleeding gashes on my shoulders. Those
were the wounds of passion.

I was important to her.

Terribly important.

I could feel it.

Westwood said, "Hey, Deston, we're here," and I returned to reality with a twinge of regret.

The scene was much the same as it had been during my previous visit, except that the new tower listed to port. At least twenty degrees.

Westwood said, "You laying odds?"

I said, "Against what?"

Westwood said, "Against the goddam thing falling down before we leave here."

I said, "Hell, it may fall down before we get out of the truck."

Lester Critchlow was on the scene. He was looking at Reverend Dawson's map of Heaven. He was shaking his head. He said, "It's completely wrong." He began to point out spots on the crumpled old paper. He said, "The pearly gates is here, not there. That manna stand is over in this here commercially zoned area. My God, Dawson, you can't open a manna stand where there is residences."

Dawson said, "You can if you is Josiah. Josiah got a special permit. It was all explained in my vision." He placed his hands on his hips. He said, "Now you run along on account of I got me a tower to build."

Critchlow said, "You ain't never gonna get no tower built till you switches to brick and mortar."

Westwood grabbed my arm. He said, "Holy Christ, look out, here she comes! Run for your goddam life!"

I started to run and my game leg folded under me. Westwood picked me up like I was a rag doll. The big man could really move. The falling tower missed us by inches. I said, "Thanks, Constable. What can I do in return?"

Westwood said, "Well, you might autygraph a old baseball I got at home."

I said, "I'd be glad to."

Westwood said, "Ain't often you get the autygraph of a feller what hit into five straight double plays."

t was shortly before noon. I was in my room banging out my resignation from the *Globe* and wondering what I'd do with twenty-five grand a year and all that free time. I thought I'd probably have a shot at the baseball book I'd always wanted to do. I'd call it *And Yet So Far.* I'd find my material in the guys who had spent a few days in the majors and long years in the minors, the guys who had tried and tried and failed and failed and I'd do it in rough-hewn style. The gut story of baseball is found in the heartbreak of the little man, not in the twice-a-century sagas of George Herman Ruth and Willie Howard Mays.

The phone ran. I hauled it onto the bed with me.

I said, "Hello."

Clancy said, "I hear bedsprings squeaking! You're in the hay with some buck-toothed, corn-fed young thing and I'm up here withering on the goddam vine! Why, I should kill you, you sonofabitch!"

She hung up. I shook my head and returned the phone to the nightstand.

"There is no other purgatory but a woman."

From *Scornful Lady* by Beaumont and Fletcher.

It shouldn't have taken two guys to figure that out.

Pennsy wasn't on hand for the noon meal.

Lester Critchlow showed up late with a black eye.

Stars And Stripes Forever Fogarty sat quietly at the table spinning the cylinder on his huge revolver. Every chamber was loaded. He jammed the monster into his shoulder holster and attacked the spare ribs and sauerkraut with gusto. He said, "Gotta keep my strength up. That big banzai attack gonna happen any damn night now."

Kelly Clark's ferret face was buried in his Racing Form.

Nate Jones entered carrying a tarnished old trumpet. He

placed it gently on the table. He said, "It gonna look like brand-new when I get it all shined up."

I said, "Are you a musician?"

Nate Jones said, "No, I just seen this here poor ole horn in the music store window. It looked kind of discarded and lonesome so I figured we might as well keep each other company."

Ma Stinson came in. Her big white cat was clinging to her shoulder. From the parlor the radio blared "It Wasn't God Who Made Honky Tonk Angels." Ma Stinson said, "Do you like country music, Mr. Deston?"

I said, "Yes, ma'am, I like it real well."

Lester Critchlow sneered. He said, "It's the music of the Devil. It's always about somebody climbing in bed with somebody they ain't got no business climbing in bed with."

Ma Stinson said, "Well, Mr. Critchlow, you can't deny that such things do happen." She looked at me and her eyes sparkled with good humor. She said, "Isn't that right, Mr. Deston?"

She leaned over and whispered in my ear, "Tell Chet Westwood his laundry is ready."

I whispered, "Ma'am, do you put starch in his shirt collars?"

Ma Stinson whispered, "Well, certainly. Why?"

I whispered, "I just wondered."

After the evening meal I spent my Susie Weatherby Hour on the front porch glider with a half-dozen cigarettes. I went up to my room with vague intentions of doing a foreword on the baseball thing. I wanted to head for Chicago, but my cut shoulders smarted and the night before careened around in my memory. I kept thinking about an encore. It wasn't long in coming.

My window shade was down and there was a light scent of hyacinth in the darkened room. Pennsy said, "Your door was unlocked and I hoped that might be an invitation."

She lay naked and face-down on my bed. I sat beside her

126

and eased her onto her back. I kissed her and said, "You're a brown-eyed brunette again."

Pennsy said, "Yes, I suppose I should have told you about that. The wig and lenses weren't intended for you. They're for the benefit of Bert Clangingham who doesn't have the slightest idea who I am."

I said, "You're Clangingham's partner and he doesn't know it?"

Pennsy said, "I hired out as his personal secretary under the name of Holly Comstock. I thought it might be wise to learn if my business associate-to-be is an honest man." She rolled her eyes. She said, "Which he isn't, by the way. As Eloise Henderson I couldn't possibly have made such a discovery until it was too late."

I said, "You were lucky that Clangingham just happened to need a secretary."

Pennsy shot me her quick smile. She said, "Well, you see, Clangingham needed a secretary because his old secretary received a beautiful offer from a Chicago concern."

I said, "Coincidence, of course."

Pennsy laughed her wind-chime laugh. She said, "Why, of course."

I said, "But your picture was in the papers."

Pennsy said, "Rip, you saw me every day of my trial and even you weren't positive."

I said, "Not until you spoke."

Pennsy said, "Clangingham and I had never met. I hadn't so much as spoken to him on the telephone."

She drew my head down to her bare bosom. She said, "Rip, I'm a branded woman, do you realize that?"

I said, "Yes, and a mad-dog Chicago newspaper reporter did the dirty job."

Pennsy ran her fingers back and forth through my iron-gray crew cut. She said, "He erred and wist it not, and it shall be forgiven him."

I said, "Bible?"

Pennsy said, *"Leviticus."*

My hand traveled across her flat, tight stomach. Pennsy watched its progress. She lay unmoving except to spread her legs ever so slightly. The late May breeze swayed the window blind and fluttered the curtains. The sounds of Ma Stinson's radio drifted up the stairs. "Teardrops in My Heart." There was a faint tremor in Pennsy's lovely lower-half. She gasped once sharply and began to squirm in a gently rotating fashion. She said, "Rip, are you having a good time down there?"

I said, "Damn right."

Pennsy said, "I hope you aren't starting something you won't finish."

I said, "So do I "

Pennsy said, "Then we should stop talking."

I said, "Suits me."

I was on my second flapjack drenched in maple syrup when Constable Westwood tapped me on the shoulder. I grabbed the table and held on, I took a swig of Ma Stinson's excellent coffee and said, "Yes?"

Westwood said, "There ain't no use in us going out there this morning. The tower just fell down again."

I said, "Any serious damage?"

Westwood said, "Just to Dawson's pride."

I said, "This could go on all summer."

Westwood said, "Maybe not. Critchlow just talked Dawson into going with brick and mortar." He stepped back and looked at me. He said, "How did your face get all cut up like that?"

I said, "Dull razor blade."

That morning I sat on the glider and went through half-a-pack of cigarettes. I watched the big red trucks roll into Catastrophe, Missouri. On the door of every truck was a large sign. LESTER CRITCHLOW BRICK AND MORTAR. GOPHER CENTER, MISSOURI.

n this particular twilight I wasn't thinking about
Susie Weatherby. I cuddled Pennsy to me and
said, "So tell me all about Sigmund Freud."

Pennsy threw an impossibly beautiful leg across my belly.
There was a sly little smile in her voice. She said, "Somehow
the name fails to ring a bell. He must have been a bum lay."

I said, "Well, he has to be around here somewhere. What
the hell have you been doing in bed with a guy twice your
age?"

Pennsy giggled. She said, "Good God, you don't remember?"

I said, "Stop, look, and listen, will you? You're talking to the damn fool who did his best to destroy you."

Pennsy said, "What was his name?"

I said, "Rip Deston."

Pennsy said, "Oh, yes, the big man with the crew cut who leaves me panting. Is that the one?"

I said, "If he has a nasty bite on his neck, he's the one."

Pennsy propped herself up on an elbow. She said, "Look, Rip, let's call it a draw. I've been crazy about you since I got hooked on your head-on-collision writing. Can't you understand that?"

I said, "Hell, no."

Pennsy said, "I've read nearly everything you've done in recent years. I mean everything from high school basketball to restaurant fires to the murder trial of a star-crossed little bitch by the name of Eloise Henderson. All of it was earnest. Not always accurate, but straight-from-the-shoulder honest. Can you imagine what that means to a woman?"

I said, "I haven't the foggiest."

Pennsy said, "Well, it means that she's found a straight-up man." She took my cigarette and turned the gray ash to ruby red. She gave it back to me and said, "Rip, you don't put on airs and you don't use big words. You're neither cute nor exceptionally clever. You just come on straight as a string."

I said, "That's important?"

Pennsy said, "Lover, that's so important I can taste it." She grinned and came back to her pillow. She said, "All right, let me not even attempt an explanation."

I said, "Your explanation would probably be over my head anyway."

Pennsy said, "Of course it would, but don't ever.short-change yourself." She gave me a quick peck on the cheek and whispered, "Darling," into my ear. Her hyacinth perfume surged in my brain.

I stared at Ma Stinson's busted ceiling. I said, "Well, this would make one helluva book."

Pennsy said, "Then write it, but give me a chance to grind my personal axe."

I said, "I knew it was too good to be true."

Pennsy's wind-chime laughter rippled through the dimness. She said, "How would you like to be editor of the *Globe?*"

I said, "I just *resigned* from the *Globe.*"

Pennsy said, "I know you did but I'll rehire you as top-dog the moment I get back to Chicago. I want a lay-it-on-the-line publication and you're the man who can give it to me."

I said, "How will Clangingham take that?"

Pennsy said, "Does it matter? I'll have fifty-one percent."

I said, "I must be dreaming."

Pennsy said, "Do I bluff?"

I shook my head.

Pennsy said, "All right, next week Sam Cohen gets his walking papers and you're the new high lama." She gave me a cunning wink. She said, "On one condition."

I said, "Oh-oh."

Pennsy said, "I want to be Mrs. Rip Deston."

I said, "My God."

Pennsy said, "I mean it. I'll make you happier than Clancy could."

I said, "How do you know about Clancy?"

Pennsy said, "Oh, once in a while Marty would drop a

tidbit." She sat up. She spun around and tickled my chin with her toes. The view was tremendous, even in the dim light. She said, "Deal?"

I was in love and when you're in love you can't find a no in your vocabulary.

I said, "Deal."

Pennsy said, "Now come here to me."

I did and she bit the other side of my neck.

I winced.

Pennsy said, "You drive me crazy."

There comes a time in the dead of night when the tides recede and the sleep of man is best. It is the hour of the good sleep, the satisfying sleep, the sleep that nourishes the body and rekindles spent fires. Man does not stir nor does he dream. He breathes with the eternal precision of planetary movement. It is the sleep of sleeps and I was torn from the comfort of its womb by a sound out of the sulphur-choked recesses of the great fiery hole. It was the shriek of the great grandmother of all demons. I gasped, "Good Christ, what is it?" I bounded from the bed and groped for my robe.

Pennsy grabbed at me and missed. She said, "Rip, come back, it's only somebody blowing a fish-horn."

I bolted from the room just in time to see Ma Stinson fall stark-naked down the stairs.

Her big white cat hissed and clawed at me from the sanctuary of the hallway chandelier.

Kelly Clark stumbled into the hall carrying his Racing Form and yelling, "Oh, my God, they're at the post!"

Lester Critchlow burst upon the scene in his underwear sans undershirt. He waved his Bible aloft and shouted, "At last the King has come!"

A door flew open and Stars And Stripes Forever Fogarty appeared in his underwear sans shorts. His horse-pistol was held at the ready and he bellowed, "Banzai, my ass!" He opened fire at nothing in particular.

The chandelier came down with a great shattering sound to leave Ma Stinson's cat suspended snarlingly from its severed chain.

Ma Stinson came reeling wild-eyed up the stairs. She was clad in her parlor drapes. She groaned, "Pray, you fools, pray!"

One door remained closed. Through it poured the unearthly screams of a tarnished old trumpet.

Nate Jones was having his moment.

It was eight o'clock in the morning and I was waiting for Constable Westwood to drive me to the railroad station.

I sat with Pennsy on Ma Stinson's front porch steps watching Nate Jones walk dejectedly from the boarding house. There was an olive-drab duffel bag slung over his shoulder. He carried a battered suitcase in one hand and in the other was a blindingly-bright trumpet.

Ma Stinson was nailing a ROOM FOR RENT sign to a porch pillar.

Pennsy said, "What in the world will happen to that poor man?"

Ma Stinson said, "He got a room over at Clara Miller's place." She brandished her hammer over her head. She said, "Maybe Clara can handle him but she don't make apple dumplings worth a damn."

Pennsy moved closer to me. She said, "Do you love me?"

I said, "You know I do."

Pennsy said, "How much?"

I said, "All I've got."

Pennsy looked down at the toes of her white pumps and wiggled them nervously. She said, "Rip, I've had bad breaks and I've made mistakes. I've stripped for lechers and I threw my virginity away at an early age. If you're looking for an angel you're on the wrong porch with the wrong woman but, Rip, on my dead mother's soul, I swear I love you! I want to be yours and I want you to be mine! God, think of the life we can have together!"

I said, "Has it ever occurred to you that I could be in a wheelchair by the time you're fifty?"

Pennsy said, "Of course, but has it ever entered your mind that I would be proud to push your wheelchair?"

The constable's pickup truck stopped in front of the house. Westwood glanced at his watch and pointed to it. I waved my acknowledgment.

I grabbed my stuff and we went out to the truck.

Pennsy grabbed me and kissed me. She bit my lower lip until it bled. She said, "I'll be in Chicago within a week. I couldn't stand a moment more than that without you."

I climbed into the truck and slammed the door. I said, "I'll call you every day."

Pennsy put her head through the window. She said, "You'd

better!" She kissed me on the cheek and said, "Sweetheart, when I get back a pair of Ohioans are going to give Chicago a new *Globe* newspaper!"

I said, "Who's the other Ohioan?"

Pennsy put a thumb to her marvelous chest in a gesture of mock self-importance. She said, "Why, me, of course."

I said, "You're from Pennsylvania."

Pennsy said, "Oh, yes, I was raised there but I was born in Ohio. I'm an orphan, Rip. I never knew my real father's name and my stepfather was killed in the war. My mother died when I was fourteen months old."

I said, "Kiddo, you certainly know how to roll with the punches."

Pennsy said, "It's all right now. Now I have you."

I said, "Just where in Ohio were you born?"

Pennsy said, "My birthday was July 9th of '42 and the calamity took place in a town by the name of Cornelius. My stepfather's name was Henderson and my mother's maiden name was Weatherby. Susan Weatherby, God rest her soul."

Constable Westwood checked his watch. He said, "I think we better travel." He drove away from Ma Stinson's and when we turned toward the railroad station I didn't look back. I knew that Pennsy would be waving goodbye.

Westwood said, "I see you got your neck all chewed up." He said, "Deston, you're getting out of town in the nick of time."

I said, "Constable, pull over first chance you get."

Westwood said, "How come?"

I wiped blood from my mouth.

I said, "I'm sick to my stomach."

Westwood said, "You better make it snappy. We're running late."

A few minutes later he said, "A sweet young dish like that Miss Comstock can do awful things to a feller your age. Hell, you're old enough to be her father."

The joy and laughter were gone.

My bluebird of happiness had flapped away on giant ebony wings. I staggered through June and July, drunkenly trying to sidestep three days of my life.

No way.

The memories lashed me mercilessly.

I didn't have the guts to call Pennsy and lay it on the line and Pennsy didn't call me.

I wondered if she had stumbled onto the fact that she'd been in bed with her father.

I hoped not.

She'd been through enough.

Rain swept the city like a great gray broom and Angelo's was nearly deserted. Clancy sat in a booth and glared at her watch. She said, "You're late again."

I ordered a double Clinch Mountain and drank it in sips, washing it around in my mouth, savoring it, and looking at the yellowed interior view of the Roman Coliseum.

The fat accordion player dozed at a table, his instrument on the floor beside him. His hair was snow white now. I lit a cigarette and sat in stony silence. I was a million years old.

Clancy watched me the way a bank cop watches a guy with an empty shopping bag. She said, "For God's sake, Rip, what's the matter with you? What the hell happened in that rotten little town?"

I caught the eye of the waitress and pointed to my empty glass.

Clancy said, "You've been back for ten weeks and you haven't drawn a sober breath. You always need a shave, your suit looks like a pawnshop special and your socks haven't matched in a month."

I said, "Clancy, just forget it."

Clancy said, "Forget it, my ass! Aren't you ever going back to work?"

I said, "Not at the *Globe.*"

Clancy said, "Were you fired?"

I said, "No, I resigned."

Clancy said, "*Why,* for God's sake?"

I said, "You wouldn't believe me if I told you."

Clancy said, "So what are you going to do now?"

I shrugged and said, "I wish I knew."

Rain roared on Angelo's flat roof. Clancy said, "I've had it with you, Rip." She meant it, I could tell. Well, that was okay with me. She'd do all right. She was tough and worldly-wise and with her feline instincts she was a cinch to come down on her feet. Clancy wasn't important anymore. Nothing was important.

I said, "Sorry, Clancy. Maybe I need a doctor."

Clancy said, "I know damn well you do. You just missed Bannister's doctor. He comes in a couple times a week with his bitchy little receptionist. You should get an appointment."

I said, "With Schnickenfish?"

Clancy said, "With *who?*"

I said, "Bannister's doctor. Schnickenfish. Felix Schnick-enfish."

Clancy said, "What are you talking about? His name is Milo Gortman. He'll cost you an arm and a leg, but he's top-drawer. Who the hell is Felix Schnickenfish?"

The tiniest of sparks flickered to life in the depths of my dying mind. Clancy stared at me. She said, "Rip, what's wrong? You're pale. What did I say?"

I left the booth and blundered through the tables to the door.

I plunged into the driving rain.

Home.

The only four-letter word that makes any sense.

The narrow macadam road and the familiar sights that quicken the pulse.

The broken-down red barn on the left with its faded old Mail Pouch sign. The cut-rate gas station on the right, closed now, pumps rusted out, weeds choking the drive. When the world was young, I had applied for a job there.

Now the trees arched over Cornelius Road and my bus swept into the long, green tunnel to yesterday. I jerked my handkerchief from my pocket. Lord, I was coming home after more than twenty-seven years.

I left the bus in front of Perry's Sporting Goods, Newsstand, Soda Fountain, and Delicatessen late on that golden afternoon. I dropped my suitcase and typewriter and looked around. Cornelius seemed much smaller than I remembered it but I saw no important changes. The pool room had been rebuilt as a laundromat. Some painting had been done but not enough to matter. The streets were still red brick, the sidewalks were still cracked to form the same old designs, the curbing was still broken in the same old places. A tattered flag still flew from the drug store roof. Forty-eight stars, not fifty. Frank Miller had always resisted change.

I took my things into Perry's. Rudy Perry was wiping the soda fountain counter. He was completely bald now. I said, "Hi, Rudy."

Rudy said, "Hi, Rip. Seen you get off the bus. You been out of town?"

I said, "Yeah, for a while."

Rudy said, "You must of sprained your ankle. You got a bad limp."

I said, "It's nothing I can't live with." I sat on a chipped white-enameled stool and hooked my heels to its triangular foot-rest. I ordered a cherry Coke. I said, "Rudy, can I leave my stuff here for a few hours?"

Rudy said, "Sure, Rip, we don't close until way up around nine."

I said, "I have to find out about Susie Weatherby."

Rudy served my cherry Coke and we talked.

limped south on Creek Road. Three-quarters of a mile and the sidewalk ended. I followed the cinder path down through the gully and over the creek bridge. I climbed the long, gradual hill, head down, lost in thought.

I'd been over those same cinders thousands of times. To school, to the library, to the pool room, to the ball field. But not to the grocery store. The grocery store was up on East Hill and I'd cut through the East Hill Cemetery to get there. Except after dark, of course. My first job had been in the East Hill Cemetery. Mowing grass. One buck per day. No power mowers in those days.

I could see the house a hundred yards ahead. Still white and trimmed in green with stained glass panels above the dining room window and a sagging front porch where you could sit at night and watch lightning bugs and listen to crickets under big copper moons and count stars that actually twinkled.

I stopped in front of the old house. The apple tree was still standing. I could see the pump at the rear door. Painted silver now. It had been black when I was a kid. I peered back through the wooded eight acres. There was a stream out there. I had spent many an afternoon on its banks with Baskerville. Baskerville had been a spotted dog that came to dinner and stayed until he died.

The memories swarmed like a cloud of honey bees until a well-built woman stepped onto the sagging front porch where an old swing hung on rusty chains.

She said, "Are you looking for someone, sir?"

I said, "I used to live here. A long time ago."

The woman peered at me. She said, "You did? When was that?"

I said, "Before the war. I sold to the Merriams."

The woman threw her hands to her face. She said, "Oh, dear God, Rip, is that you?"

I said, "Yeah, Sooz, it's me."

Susie and I sat facing each other in front of the glazed brick fireplace. I said, "Rudy Perry told me you were here."

Susie made no reply. She huddled in her chair as if she had a chill. Her hands shook almost uncontrollably. I said, "Sooz, there's a bottle in my suitcase but the damn thing's down at Perry's."

Susie said, "I think I have something in the kitchen." She got up and walked unsteadily in that direction. She had gained an inch at the waist but this had been beautifully balanced by two or three at the bust. She was still slim-legged. There were lines in her face but they were soft lines. Her cornsilk hair had escaped autumn's early frost. Her cornflower eyes were clear and gentle and there were smile crinkles at their corners.

We nipped at little glasses of Old Anchor Chain and I looked around. The walls had been painted beige and a china cabinet had been built into a corner of the dining room but the window seat remained and the hardwood floors were brightly polished. Susie said, "I bought the place when the Merriams moved to Florida twelve years ago. It's too big for a woman living alone but I simply had to have it. I guess you might say it was an obsession."

I said, "Do I know why, Sooz?"

Susie gazed into the dead fireplace and shrugged. She said, "Of course. My very best memories are here." She looked up with tears in her eyes. She said, "Aw, Rip, what happened?"

I said, "There was a war, Sooz."

Susie said, "I know. My gosh, I ought to know. It cost me my lover and it made me a widow in less than ten months. Don't tell me about the war."

I held a match to Susie's trembling cigarette. Through the smoke she said, "Rip, I never heard from you." There was no accusation in her voice. Just uncomprehending wonder.

I said, "Sooz, I wrote a couple of times but maybe the boats got sunk." It was a lie but it was lily-white.

Susie studied the coal of her cigarette.

I said, "I heard you were married and later on I heard you were dead." That was the truth. It was just turned around a bit.

Susie said, "No, Rip, I wasn't dead but for a long time I wished I was."

I nodded. I said, "I know the feeling, Sooz."

S

usie drove a nondescript old Chevrolet. Not particularly well. I said, "Sooz, you'd better get
your steering fixed."

Susie said, "What for? This car goes approximately where I
aim it."

I said, "Well, about half the time you're aiming it in the
wrong goddam direction."

Susie said, "Rip, this is the best handling car I've ever had."
I didn't say anything.

Susie said, "Power steering, you know."
I still didn't say anything.

I picked up my suitcase and typewriter at Perry's and we

headed for Murphy's Barn. We passed the East Hill Grocery Store. We passed Ricker's Strawberry Farm. We damn near passed Murphy's Barn. Susie took the rattling Chevy into the gravel parking lot on screaming tires. She managed to get it stopped a half-inch short of a Mack tandem dump truck loaded with sand.

I got out and knelt briefly. Susie said, "What were you doing down there?"

I said, "Tying my shoe."

Susie said, "Then why were you looking at the sky?"

I said, "Well, shucks, Sooz, I can tie my shoes blindfolded."

Susie said, "But, Rip, you're wearing loafers."

I said, "I was just kidding, Sooz."

Murphy's Barn had been there since the flood. Noah's flood. You could see fireflies through the chinks in the walls and stars through the shingles. There wasn't a straight board in the place. In an abstract way it reminded me of Susie's driving.

We took our same old booth in the rear. I looked at the tabletop carvings and saw only a few that I didn't recognize. The place was dimmer and smokier than ever. Four truck drivers swapped tall stories at the splintered old bar and the jukebox played Bing Crosby's recording of "Serenade in the Night."

We had deluxe hamburgers and frosted steins of beer. Susie wanted to know about my limp and I told her. Then I said, "Sooz, I have to ask a question."

Susie said, "Not now, Rip. Let me enjoy this. It's so much like old times."

We chatted. Susie was working in the office at the furniture store. I said, "What furniture store?"

Susie said, "Where the candy shop opened after the real estate office moved over to Delancey Street."

I said, "I see." I really didn't.

Susie gave me all the breathtaking news. Rod Harshberger had married Betty Vrable in '46. It had been one hell of a wedding. Rod Harshberger's mother had slugged the preacher. They had been divorced two months ago. It had been one hell of a divorce. Rod Harshberger's mother had slugged the judge.

Windy Rubington had moved to Canfield. Right near the County Fair Grounds. He liked it except when the wind was from the south during the fairs. All those animals, you know. Susie giggled. She said, "Can't you just imagine?"

I told Susie yes I could just imagine.

Florence Roberts had shot a prowler in the shoulder three years ago. Before it was over Florence had dumped her husband and moved in with the prowler. Susie frowned. She said, "Isn't that strange?"

I told Susie yes that was strange.

I played the primitive twelve-selection jukebox. "Blue Hawaii" and "Deep Purple." I said, "Sooz, that jukebox is the same and so are the records."

Susie said, "Oh, no, Rip! They've replaced 'Whispering Grass' with 'To Each His Own' by Eddy Howard." Susie squinted at me. She said, "Didn't you notice 'To Each His Own' by Eddy Howard?"

I told Susie I hadn't noticed "To Each His Own" by Eddy Howard.

We had another beer and Susie wanted to know what I was doing for a living.

I said, "Nothing right now. I worked for a Chicago newspaper until late in May."

Susie said, "Did you drive a truck?"

I said, "No, I wrote."

Susie said, "I've never seen a Chicago newspaper. What do they look like?"

I said, "Pretty much the same as any other newspaper."

Susie said, "I can't picture you as a writer. That must be what your typewriter's for."

I said, "Yes."

Susie said, "What did you write?"

I said, "A bit of everything. I liked baseball best."

Susie said, "You would."

A truck driver came to our booth. He said, "Hey, Susie-Q, let's dance."

Susie said, "No."

The truck driver said, "Aw, come on, Susie-Q, we always dance."

Susie said, "Don't be silly. I've never seen you before in my life."

The truck driver went away looking puzzled.

Susie said, "Do you know that we've never spent a full night together?"

I said, "We should try that sometime."

Susie clapped her hands happily. She said, "Oh, Rip, I'm so glad you thought of that."

stopped at the backdoor pump. I pumped with my right hand and drank from the palm of my left hand. The water was bitter cold with a clean iron taste. Just as I remembered it. I wiped my mouth and discovered that my typewriter and suitcase were missing. So was Susie.

I found my typewriter at the foot of the stairs. I found my suitcase in front of Susie's bedroom closet. I found Susie in bed. She wasn't wearing a stitch. In a few minutes she was moaning, "Oh, SHINE on HAR-vest MOON!" and "Out OUT brief CAN-dle!" and "Oh, welcome HOME, Rip, Rip, RIP!"

Then she lay close to me. Her cornsilk hair fluttered gently in the currents of my breathing. Her contented sigh floated across twenty-seven long, lonely years. I blew lightly into her ear. Susie jumped a foot. She said, "I just knew that was coming! You always do that, damn you!" She giggled and I stroked her thigh until she closed her eyes and purred.

I said, "Sooz, you're better than ever. You've been practicing."

Susie opened one cornflower eye.

She said, "So have you."

Susie tilted my bottle of Clinch Mountain. She brought it down in a hurry. She coughed and sputtered and shuddered. She said, "Oh, my God, give me a cigarette! This stuff is atrocious!"

I said, "How can it be atrocious? It costs eight bucks a quart."

Susie said, "So does deck varnish and you can't drink that either!"

We sat naked and cross-legged in the middle of the bed.

We had been staring at each other, trying to believe. Susie touched my bad leg tenderly. She said, "Rip, that's a shame."

I said, "It doesn't matter anymore. Hell, Sooz, I'm going on fifty."

Susie said, "Does it hurt?"

I said, "Not enough to notice. It's mostly numb but it gets me around pretty well."

Susie said, "Rip, what are you doing in Cornelius after all the years?"

I said, "That's easy. You."

Susie said, "No, Rip, that doesn't rhyme. You'd heard I was dead, remember?"

I said, "Yes, I'd heard it but I finally had to come back to see for myself. Sooz, you've been on my mind."

Susie said, "Who told you I was dead?"

I said, "Oh, it was sort of a grapevine thing. Somebody who knew somebody who knew somebody."

Susie said, "Recently?"

I said, "Sooz, it seems like a hundred years ago."

It did.

Susie said, "Rip, I hate to look a gift horse in the mouth but are you married?"

I said, "No, Sooz, not married and not divorced. Didn't you ever inquire about me? War Department or anything?"

Susie said, "Oh, God, certainly not! I preferred not knowing. I'd have lost no matter what I learned. If you'd been killed in action it would have destroyed me and if you'd thrown me over it would have broken my heart. Do you know what I mean?"

I nodded. I said, "Can I ask my question now?"

Susie said, "Look, if it's about my getting married there was a special reason."

I said, "That isn't it."

I took a deep breath and said, "Sooz, did you ever have a baby? I mean with me?"

Susie looked away from me. She nodded very slowly. She said, "That was why I married Gary Henderson. To give the baby a name."

Henderson. My God.

Susie said, "Gary was killed on Guadalcanal in September of '42."

I was silent. There might be one last-ditch roll left in the dice. Just one. I said, "Boy or girl, Sooz?"

Susie said, "Girl. On a cloudy Thursday morning at nine thirty-three. July 9th."

I could feel my stomach begin to disengage from my body.

Susie said, "Eloise has been gone such a long time."

I said, "Eloise?"

Susie nodded. She said, "Blonde and blue-eyed and sweeter than the dickens. Oh, Rip, you'd have loved every inch of her!"

I thought, good Christ, Sooz, if you only knew how I've loved every inch of her.

I sat in mute misery. Tried and condemned for the foulest crime on the face of God's green earth. I had to say something. I said, "Where is she now, Sooz?"

Susie looked at me strangely. She swallowed hard. She tried to speak and failed. She got it out the second time around. She said, "Rip, she's in East Hill Cemetery. She died at fourteen months."

Susie came apart at the seams like a sixty-cent baseball. She dropped face-down on the bed. Her body was convulsed by sobs.

Tears began to flow from my eyes.

A scalding flood of joy.

My only child was dead.

curled a blanket over Susie's bare shoulders. I sat
on the edge of the bed and lit a cigarette. I tried
to reconstruct the vendetta of the century.

Webster's New Collegiate Dictionary defines revenge as
"an act or instance of retaliating in order to get even." Well,
Pennsylvania Woods could have told Webster a few things
about revenge. Hers was a shot from Edgar Allan Poe. It was
hideously twisted. It writhed in its own green venom.

Pennsy had slipped the noose around my neck by taking me
to bed and she had sprung the trap with those final eight
words. . . . my mother's maiden name was Weatherby . . .
Susan Weatherby.

She had sent me staggering blindly into Hell. Inescapable Hell but for a chance remark.

And why? Good Lord, because of a series of newspaper columns that called a murder a murder.

She had been clever, but cleverness wouldn't have been enough. Circumstance and egotistical male gullibility had contributed heavily.

Why hadn't I followed up on her Doctor Felix Schnickenfish story? Simple. I had abandoned my defenses in my desire to believe the lovely young creature who had ostensibly fallen head over heels in love with the man of her dreams.

Gullibility? That wasn't the right word. Stupidity was more like it. Women with Pennsy's ammunition don't shoot it up on fifty-year-old, drunken, lame, two-bit reporters. But contacting Schnickenfish wouldn't have helped. I had no doubt that Schnickenfish was some sort of licensed physician and that Pennsy had paid him well for his cooperation. He would have thrown me medical curve balls concerning my father's fictitious leukemia and I would have struck out on three pitches.

How had she acquired such an arsenal of information? I hadn't told her anything. I hadn't so much as mentioned Cornelius, Ohio. My father hadn't dropped "once-in-a-while tidbits." He had given Pennsy every damned detail of my life. He had known about Susie and the baby. As a wealthy newspaper owner he possessed the equipment to check on the matter and as my father he had been interested enough to use it. And he hadn't wanted to hurt me by giving me the facts.

Who *was* Eloise Henderson alias Pennsylvania Woods alias Holly Comstock alias God knows who? Well, she'd been my father's private roll in the hay back when he was still capable of rolling in the hay and she'd moved into his life like the camel into the Arab's tent. He had supplied her with the name of his dead granddaughter and he had seen no harm in the move. Pennsy's coloring had been right, her age was close enough, and he knew that a deceased infant doesn't protest when its identity is assumed by a woman in another part of the country. Undoubtedly the name had served to sever Pennsy's connection with a sordid past. Whoever she was there was no telling what she might have done along her crooked road.

Why hadn't I checked out her story of Susie's death? Pennsy had gambled, but the odds had been heavily in her favor. It wasn't likely that I would return to a town I had spurned for twenty-seven years to howl at the grave of the woman I had abandoned in her pregnancy. Only the wildest of coincidences could have brought that about. A coincidence like Clancy knowing the name of my father's doctor.

Pennsy had beaten a murder rap, gained controlling interest in one of the country's major newspapers and, carrying the role of Eloise Henderson just a step further, she had cost me the last job I'd ever have. By baiting me with sex and a trust fund that probably didn't exist, she had all but destroyed the man who had ripped her mask away. And one of these days old Bert Clangingham would drop dead and she'd own the *Chicago Globe* right down to its last drum of ink. Clangingham didn't figure to last much longer.

Clangingham! Jesus Christ, Clangingham!

I said, "Sooz, I have to make a very important long distance telephone call! It's hotter than a three-dollar pistol!"

Susie said, "The phone's on the nightstand." She reached over and slapped my good leg and said, "Take your time and regain your strength. You're going to need it."

said, "Constable Westwood, this is Rip Deston."
Westwood said, "Who?"

I said, "The reporter from Chicago. The guy with the gimpy leg."

Westwood said, "Yeah, well, I guess you heard. I want you to know that I'm sorry but there ain't nothing I can do about it."

I said, "Sorry about what?"

Westwood said, "About arresting your girl friend for pushing ole Bert Clangingham off that crazy tower to Heaven."

I said, "Good God, is he dead?"

Westwood said, "Well, I reckon he's dead. He landed head-first in the brick pile. They had that damn tower up to near a hunnert foot at the time. It didn't fall over till they got 'er up to one-fifteen."

I said, "What the hell happened?"

Westwood said, "I was out there just nosing around after dark and I heard this awful sound like some goddam Swiss yodeler or something and right about then ole Bert hit the brick pile. I shone my flashlight up on that staircase they got going around and around and I seen Miss Comstock up there almost all the way to the top. I hollered for her to come down and she did and she told me Bert Clangingham fell off. I asked her what they was doing up there in the first place and she said all she knowed was Clangingham asked her to go up there with him."

I said, "Did you see Miss Comstock push him?"

Westwood said, "Hell, no, I didn't know there was anybody up there till ole Bert hit the brick pile."

I said, "You'll never make it stick."

Westwood said, "Yes, we will. Stars And Stripes Fogarty been going up on the tower every night to watch for that big Japanese banzai attack. He was only five foot away when she shoved Bert off."

I said, "So what happens now?"

Westwood said, "Well, she got some hotshot lawyer coming down from Chicago tomorrow. Name of Stirrups Richey or something."

I gave Westwood Susie's name and telephone number and asked if he'd call collect if anything developed.

Westwood said, "Sure thing. It won't cost nothing but time and I can sure afford that."

I hung up and Susie said, "Who is Miss Comstock?"

I said, "Sooz, I wish to Christ I knew."

The lights were out and I was trying to sleep.

Susie said, "When the Merriams moved into this house they thought I was in touch with you and I was ashamed to admit that I wasn't."

I said, "Yeah, well, goodnight, Sooz."

Susie said, "Rip, they gave me a box of old letters they found in a corner of the attic."

I said, "Letters?"

Susie said, "I hope you'll forgive me for reading them about a thousand times. They're beautiful. Oh, my God, Rip, did he ever love her!" There was genuine awe in Susie's voice. As though she was standing at the edge of Grand Canyon.

I said, "Sooz, it's a bit late at night to be making riddles."

Susie said, "I'm talking about letters from your father to your mother during World War I. I liked to pretend they were from you to me during World War II."

My mind was staggering. Out of the frying pan into the fire. I was beginning to feel like Custer at the Little Big Horn. I said, "What about the letters?"

Susie said, "Oh, they start out coming from Camp Sherman, Ohio, and then they're from France. There are over two hundred and they're like a beautiful, funny, sad story. Your father and his buddy certainly got into a lot of mischief."

I said, "His buddy?"

She said, "Marty Bannister. One night they found a stray cow and they shooed it into the cooks' tent. Things like that."

I said, "Marty Bannister?"

Susie said, "Yes, they were very close. They even had a pact."

I said, "Pact? What kind of pact?"

She said, "Well, in case one of them got killed the survivor would sort of look after the other's family. Wasn't that nice of them, Rip?"

I said, "Very nice."

She said, "Of course your mother didn't need help because of your father's investments and all."

I said, "We were very well provided for."

Susie cuddled up close and said, "Goodnight, Rip. Please don't blow in my ear."

I said, "I won't, Sooz."

couldn't go to sleep. I said, "By God, I ought to write a book."

Susie sat up and lit two cigarettes. She handed one to me. She said, "Fiction?"

I shrugged. I said, "Not exactly."

Susie asked, "Will you give me a copy?"

I answered, "I'll have to write it first."

Susie didn't say a word but her cigarette flared brightly in the dark room. In a moment she put it out and dropped onto her pillow.

She tossed and turned.

She sat up and lit another cigarette.

She said, "Rip, Cornelius might be a good place to write a book. It's so quiet and everything."

I said, "Yeah, but I've been gone so long I don't know anybody anymore."

Susie said, "You know me."

I said, "I would need a place to stay."

She said, "How long does it take to write a book?"

I said, "That's like asking how high is up. One, two, three years maybe."

She said, "I bet some people never get done."

I said, "That's right. There are more starts than finishes." I stretched and sighed. I said, "Well, it's just an idea."

Susie lit another cigarette. I said, "Sooz, you haven't finished your last cigarette."

She said, "Oh, gracious! Here, you smoke this one." Her hands trembled.

The silence was heavy. At last Susie said, "Rip, you could stay here if you wanted. You could use the other bedroom for writing. There's an old desk in there." She was talking faster and faster. She said, "I could buy a new rug. I get a discount on rugs. I could put up new curtains and things. I'd get you a desk chair. I'd get a discount on that, too. I'm really a very quiet woman, Rip. Most of the time I hardly even know I'm around."

I said, "Would I be too much trouble, Sooz?"

Susie's lamp clicked on. She popped out of bed.

I said, "Where the hell would I sleep?"

Susie said, "Boy, for a guy who wants to write a book you don't have much imagination." She grabbed my suitcase and emptied it onto the bed. She began to put my shirts on hangers, inspecting each one with an expert's frown.

She made a face. She said, "These certainly need attention."

I said, "Well, they got wrinkled in the suitcase."

Susie said, "That's not the point. There isn't a bit of starch in the collars."

The windows had grayed with dawn. Susie said, "Rip."

I said, "Wumph." It was the best I could do at that hour.

Susie said, "Could I be in your book? I'll take any old role. I'll even be the villain."

I said, "Sooz, I already have a villain."

Susie said, "Well, I just thought I'd ask."

I said, "But you'll be in the book."

Susie wiggled with delight. She said, "Oh, that's wonderful. What part will I be in?"

I said, "This part, Sooz, You'll be in this part."

It was probably the most beautiful morning since the dawn of time. Susie's coffee was a steaming masterpiece and the day's first cigarette was the best of my life. I sat at the dining room table paging through the Muddleville Gazette and listening to Susie bustling happily in the kitchen. The fragrance of sizzling bacon filled the house and ten o'clock sunshine flooded the stained glass panels of the window seat.

Being alive was a new and indescribably wonderful experience.

Susie said, "Rip, do you want more coffee?"

I said, "Damn right."

Susie filled my cup and kissed me on the back of my neck. She said, "Oh, God, am I dreaming?" Her cornflower eyes were misty.

I said, "I hope not."

On the lawn several squirrels played Keystone Kops. I watched a streak of flame descend to the old apple tree and materialize into a cardinal. In the distance crows discussed at length those matters that crows have always discussed at length. These were undoubtedly the progeny of crows I had heard as a youngster.

Well, I had made the big swing. The idiotic full circle. The great zero. Only echoes remained.

The telephone jingled and Susie went into the parlor to pick it up. She said, "Rip, it's for you."

I took the phone.

Constable Westwood said, "Didn't mean to trouble you none."

I said, "Constable, my troubles are behind me."

Westwood said, "Miss Comstock just got released on bond. I told her where you was and she said as how I should give you a message."

I said, "I can just imagine. Well, tell her I just got back from that place."

Westwood said, "I don't know nothing about that. Reckon as how she had something more important in mind."

I said, "Such as?"

Westwood said, "Such as her being almost three months pregnant."

He said, "Hello?"

He said, "Hello? Hello, Deston?"

174

I said, "Yes, Constable?"

Westwood said, "Look, Deston, it don't make no matter what Miss Comstock done. You got your own conscience to worry about. You better help her out."

Westwood said, "Hello?"

I said, "Yeah, I'm here."

Westwood said, "Deston, a real man don't never walk out on a pregnant woman."